By Elswyth Thane

Fiction

RIDERS OF THE WIND
ECHO ANSWERS
CLOTH OF GOLD
HIS ELIZABETH
BOUND TO HAPPEN
QUEEN'S FOLLY
TRYST
REMEMBER TODAY
FROM THIS DAY FORWARD
MELODY
THE LOST GENERAL
LETTER TO A STRANGER

The Williamsburg Novels

DAWN'S EARLY LIGHT
YANKEE STRANGER
EVER AFTER
THE LIGHT HEART
KISSING KIN
THIS WAS TOMORROW
HOMING *(in preparation)*

Non-Fiction

THE TUDOR WENCH
YOUNG MR. DISRAELI
ENGLAND WAS AN ISLAND ONCE
THE BIRD WHO MADE GOOD
RELUCTANT FARMER

Plays

THE TUDOR WENCH
YOUNG MR. DISRAELI

Letter to a Stranger

Letter to a Stranger

by

ELSWYTH THANE

Duell, Sloan and Pearce · *New York*
Little, Brown and Company · *Boston* · *Toronto*

LIBRARY OF CONGRESS CATALOG CARD NO. 54-11130

FIRST EDITION

DUELL, SLOAN AND PEARCE—LITTLE, BROWN
BOOKS ARE PUBLISHED BY
LITTLE, BROWN AND COMPANY
IN ASSOCIATION WITH
DUELL, SLOAN & PEARCE, INC.

Published simultaneously in Canada
by Little, Brown & Company (Canada) Limited

PRINTED IN THE UNITED STATES OF AMERICA

For

Christine Knapp

The characters in this book are entirely imaginary and bear no resemblance to any living person. There has never been a letter quite like Joanna Marshall's in the author's own mail.

Letter to a Stranger

i

THE letter had been forwarded from the publishers' office, along with half a dozen others. It was written on expensive creamy notepaper with an expensive rural Connecticut address in conventional blue type at the top. The handwriting was uneven and immature, and ran a little uphill.

It looked pretty much like a hundred other fan-letters from people who had read her books and obeyed an impulse to communicate with the woman behind the printed page.

DEAR MISS ENDICOTT [*it read*] —

I never wrote a letter like this one before, so I hope you will not dismiss it as just one of those crank things that must infest the mail of every successful author. I always read your books as soon as they are published, because I love the people you write about — I mean, if they don't exist except in your imagination, then they ought to, because the world would be better off for having them in it, and they are usually people one would like to have as one's friends.

When I saw by the reviews that your latest book was about a mother-daughter conflict, I lost no time in getting hold of it, because that seemed to strike home in my own case — except that with me it's father-trouble, which I assure you is worse. You see, I haven't any mother, and my father brought me up from a small child, and I realize now, too late, that it has ruined my life. My father being an artist — commercial, not for art's sake, he always says — he does not go to an office every day as most men do, he has a studio room at home. This means that he can supervise every minute of my life, and believe me, he does! Everything I do and wear, everything I say on the telephone, everywhere I go, even my mail, comes under his all-seeing eye and ear. And sometimes it seems as though all of it is wrong, one way or another.

But for me there is no way out, as there was for the girl in your book. I used to pray that my father would marry again, because I wanted another woman in the house to turn to, even if she wasn't my real mother. Then I prayed for him to marry again so that I would be free to live my own life. But I know now that he never will, he would rather keep me dangling here without obligations on his side, as he would owe to a woman who was his wife. That is, no need to be polite when he doesn't feel like it, or generous with money, or to provide any social life or entertainment. I don't mean I'm a Cinderella drudge, we have a daily woman in, and there seems to be plenty of money, unless I want a new coat, or a television set, or anything which doesn't interest him.

You see, Miss Endicott, there is no kind-hearted author writing my life, and so there is no happy ending in sight for me. And don't you think the solution in your book was just a teeny bit providential? Not that I don't approve of happy endings, even if it's only in a book. But as I have no aunts or sisters, and no way to shift or share the load, what can I hope for? And please don't say, like the man next door, "Tell him to go to hell, and then do as you please." That's not in any way practical, and besides, I guess I'm a coward. He has rather spectacular rages.

I realize that I shouldn't have written like this to a stranger. But I always think of you as a friend, like the people you write about, who are all so real to me. I feel as though I know you, even if you don't know me. All I really meant to say when I began was, Thank you for so many happy hours—just a sort of bread-and-butter letter for all those visits to a sunnier world, so different from the one I live in, through your books. And please go on writing them as fast as you can.

Sincerely,
JOANNA MARSHALL

Eve Endicott read that one again with a somewhat fastidious expression, trying to decide whether it was pathetic or pretty awful. She was working conscientiously through a week's accumulation of fan-mail, which she always answered personally if the writers made sense and seemed genuine. Because she did all her own manuscript typing, till her fingers staggered on the keys, her correspondence was usually hand-written for the sake of a change to a pen. Her books did not as a rule attract cranks. And more than once she had said, quote, that if people took the trouble to write to an author, either in protest or in praise, the least one could do was return a civil answer, unquote.

But that was only half the reason. Eve took satisfaction in the evidence that she, the invisible story-teller, had become tangible enough to be written to — that she existed in the minds of her readers as a human being, beyond a mere signer of autographs. Eve respected her fan-mail, and gave thought to it, and her response was not routine nor given over to a secretary. She believed that the absence of a secretary — which she could never till recently afford, anyway — between herself and her scripts, as well as between herself and her correspondents, was one reason for the warm personal relationship which her books established with her readers. Her product was hand-made. There was no production line. It was slower, but it worked better.

As her backlist lengthened and her public grew, this self-imposed letter-writing chore made inroads on her time. Every so often she set aside a morning for it — a few undictated lines each, and a signature, and a hand-addressed envelope if none was enclosed. The *postage!* her uncomprehending friends would wail at her. And the *time!* But it pleased the fans, gave them something to show, especially the younger ones, and especially those who had not requested or expected a reply. Sometimes they even began a letter by saying, "Don't bother to answer this — " But she did. Even the stupid kids who demanded the story of her life and a photograph for use in their English class, without enclosing stamps, got in reply a brief reference to *Who's Who* where the facts were. Some faithful readers wrote after each new volume, naively assuming that she would remember their former communications — and sometimes she did.

Eve lived alone in a small apartment above the Park in New York, fortunate in having a dependable colored maid who came in every day but Sunday to look after her. She had had a husband once, for a little while, before he died in the Battle of the Bulge. Sometimes it astonished her how long ago that was, and she wondered what she had done with the time since then, when it had once looked so long and empty a road ahead. A row of books in bright jackets — a safe balance at the bank — old devoted friends, and a couple of flashy episodes that came to nothing — very becoming threads of white in her short dark hair, which she did not try to conceal — no trouble with her waistline — a lot of hard work — the days went by, somehow.

She glanced now at the unexceptional name at the bottom of the letter in her hand and wrote:

Letter to a Stranger

DEAR MISS MARSHALL —

Thank you for your letter about my new book —

Miss Marshall. How old would she be, to write a letter like that? No real clue on the page itself, which was a blend of immaturity and rather amateur cynicism and — the line where bathos began was very flexible. Somehow you could not laugh at Miss Marshall, nor curl your lip at her. Something stuck out. Sincerity. People in their teens were quite likely to talk recklessly of their lives being ruined. And yet, a frustrated woman of forty might have just reached realization.

The end of the book was a bit fortuitous, Eve had always been aware of that, but she had used what seemed to her the least obvious way out. If there was one thing her regulars relied on her for, it was a reasonably comfortable conclusion to her story. Violence and the sordid dark brown details of disease and despair which were considered realism in the more heavy-handed school of novelists were not in her repertoire.

And now this tiresome Marshall woman, constant reader incorporate, accused her of finagling her solution. Then let her read Hemingway, if she wasn't satisfied. No author writing her life for her, indeed, and not guts enough to rewrite it for herself! Room for a nice platitude there, about another Author with a capital A — a line from Kipling, perhaps, was called for, depending on the age of this self-made Elizabeth Barrett Browning. Usually they began, "I am a girl sixteen years old — " or "I am a grandmother twice over — " Not this mysterious Marshall. And she had succeeded in holding Eve Endicott's attention for a space of time which would have answered three or four of the usual kind of letters from ordinary people.

Maybe this was one of those it was best to pretend one hadn't received — publishers being, God forgive us, so careless about forwarding. Nonsense. Shove something down on the paper and sign your name and get on to the next one, we've got a lot more to do.

Dear Miss Marshall —

Thank you for your letter about my new book. You seem to have quite a problem but I think [*Eve wrote with deliberate sententiousness, matching Miss Marshall's general style for her own amusement*] that everybody has at one time or another wished they could escape into the life of some character in a book — not that that is any guarantee of a happy ending these days, is it!

Perhaps [*and here she made her first mistake*] it would be a good idea to cultivate that man next door. He sounds as though he might follow through with something which did prove practical, and besides when people are high and mighty like that it is fun to call their bluff. Ask him for a job!

Sincerely,
Eve Endicott

And cheerfully unaware that now she had been and done it, Eve picked up the next letter on the pile, spidery writing on apple-green notepaper:

DEAR MISS ENDICOTT —

How nice to have another one of your delightful books. The last time I wrote you . . .

ii

THE relationship between author and publisher is often a tricky thing full of pitfalls. There are publishers who appear to hate bringing out books, in the way of the legendary first violinist who hated music to the point of tears while he played. There are Svengali publishers, who are capable of hypnotizing, cajoling, and midwifing a book out of a lazy or temperamental author. And there are publishers who are simply artful listeners.

Eve was one of the lucky Benson & Shard authors, which meant that if she wanted money in advance, legal advice, or just a luncheon date, she had only to cast herself on to the telephone and Theodore Benson would handsomely provide. Benson & Shard pampered their authors — well, anyway, the ones who paid off — and there was a general feeling round the inner circles besides that since his divorce (which was not, of course, his fault, as his friends were passionately ready to prove) Tad Benson had a more than professional interest in Eve Endicott.

She was lunching with him — just for laughs — on the day that Joanna Marshall's rebuttal arrived, and as he was always interested in fan-mail she took it along in her hand-bag. She forgot it again till the coffee had come — in a pot, so that they could linger over refills — when she heard herself saying, "I'm getting a very quick reaction by mail to this new book — and not quite what you might expect."

"Outraged women who happen to be mothers and aren't a bit like that?" he suggested, for he had been a little dubious of a storyline which was based on the premise that Mom could be wrong.

"Not so far." She began to dig round in her bag. "There was one from a girl who claimed father-trouble was worse. I answered it, as usual — Thank you for writing, and so forth — and she came right back at me today. It's fascinating — I'll never understand the way people can *unbosom* themselves to a perfect stranger!"

"You're no stranger to them, Evie. You're on their bedside tables, you put into words they haven't got the feelings they hardly knew they had, you read the crystal ball for them, you're the mirror on the wall — "

"Use all that in the blurb," she suggested rudely, and handed him Joanna Marshall's second letter. "It seems to be so hard not to make it sound as though I was a high-minded bore. Read that one, anyway. It's a daisy."

He opened it with the effect of using only the tips of his fingers — treading delicately, trespassing with exaggerated deference — and an expression of impudent amusement. Eve sat watching him with affection. He wore large, owlish spectacles with heavy dark horn-rims which were so much a part of his long, laughing face that one never thought of him without them, and they seemed not to obscure his eyes, which were a lively brown. His very brushed-looking dark hair had an almost childlike shine and wave. He was, and she had often told him so herself, too good-looking to be true, but because of the spectacles, a lifelong affliction to him, it never went to his head. His bad eyesight had preserved him from the worst of the war, and he had retained a boyish bounce which overseas experience had drained out of a good many of his contemporaries. She suspected that he was a year or two younger than she was — if that mattered.

She had often caught herself wondering what sort of woman could have found Tad hard to live with or lacking in what goes to make a good marriage. People were already saying that his ex-wife's second venture, embarked on the day after the decree, was not a success — the implication being that Tad was well out of a bad job.

In any case, Tad himself had not done any visible brooding. Eve sometimes asked herself why she wasn't heels over head in love with him herself. And of course a lot of people were left speculating why she was still a widow. Once when someone speculated out loud in her hearing, she had remarked, "Inertia," and joined in the derisive hoot of laughter which ensued. Everyone knew that she had done quite a lot of running just to stay in the same place.

Tad was concentrated now with his usual obliging singleness of mind on the letter she had handed him. Evie and her fan-mail were one of his joys. She got the damnedest letters of all the authors on his list, and it was a thing he was always meaning to go into further — the effect Eve Endicott's books had on the readers, the way she loosened people's pens.

DEAR MISS ENDICOTT [*he read*] —

I never thought you'd really answer a letter like mine, I mean from just nobody at all, and yet I suppose I wouldn't have written in the first place if I hadn't hoped you would. It brings you much closer, almost as though we had met. It's odd you should say that about the man next door — I'm afraid I gave you the wrong impression, although I'm not surprised that you seem to have sensed his importance in my life. If I told you his name it might ring a bell, as he's quite well-known in New York. You might even have met him!

At this point Tad flipped over the page to see the signature.

"Marshall?" he queried. "Where does she live?"

"Connecticut, somewhere." Eve turned the envelope, which had the address printed across the back flap. "Her father is a successful artist, I gather."

"Good Lord, *Marshall!* Is this Beaumont Marshall's daughter?"

"I don't know, is it? And who is Beaumont Marshall? Do you know him?"

"I know of him, like everybody else in that neck of the woods. What a thing! Does she go on about it?" He went to the letter with a newly quickened interest.

"You mean they live near you?"

"Near enough. That's the next town to the railway station for my place, as you'd know if you'd ever come up there. Who's this poor guy whose name would ring a bell, I wonder. What a dangerous woman."

"Well, yes — after all, she doesn't know me, or whom I might know. It could be very embarrassing to someone. But she doesn't mean it that way. I think she may be very young."

He made no reply. One eyebrow slightly elevated in delighted indiscretion now, he was galloping down the page.

The fact is [*wrote Joanna Marshall*], I've been in love with him for years. Of course I never meant him to know, but sometimes I think he suspects, and it doesn't matter anyway because it's all so hopeless. He thinks I'm just a *rabbit*, because I don't seem to be able to stand up to my father. Little does he know. You see, Miss Endicott, my father is a very charming man, very good-looking, very talented, very amusing — you're waiting for the *but,* aren't you. Well, it's not what you think — he doesn't drink. That is, not too much. He's too clever for that. Sometimes I think it would be simpler if he did. That is, you could put your finger on it then. And perhaps then you *could* tell him to go to hell.

But with my father it's different. I can remember my mother quite distinctly. She didn't die, she went away when I was ten and she never came back. And my father only laughs. I know now that she went with another man — for a while I wasn't sure about that. My father has never mentioned her since then without laughing — or at least the kind of a smile you turn on like a light, with will-power. And I understood, right from the beginning, that he laughed like that because if he didn't he would cry, and that his heart was broken.

"Oh, *no!*" Tad murmured happily at this point, and read on.

So that's why I can't leave him, or tell him to go to hell, even if I had the courage [*Miss Marshall continued, harping on it, rather.*] He has been deserted once by a woman. I think twice would kill him. He said to me that day, when he told me that she was never coming back, he said, "Well, we'll get along, won't we, baby? Let her go, there's still two of us, isn't there, baby." And he laughed. That's it, you see. There has to be two of us, for him.

For a long time I didn't mind. That is, I was proud if he needed me, like a grown up person. But now I begin to see — he had no *right*. A person should have a choice. I don't, and I can see what it's done to me, and it's too late. The harm is done, the pattern is formed. He has taken possession of my whole life. And if I tried to get away now I think he would go out of his mind.

So you see, Miss Endicott, why I take my happy endings second hand, and why I envy your characters so much. If only you could do the same for me!

Sincerely,
JOANNA MARSHALL

Tad Benson snapped the letter shut into its folds and tossed it on the tablecloth.

"That could be a very nasty little piece of work," he said, without smiling.

"Yes, but I don't think so," Eve said cautiously. "Unless perhaps they're both a bit dotty."

"Oh, Marshall's quite cracked, I don't think there's any doubt about that. I never knew there was a daughter. There's probably some excuse for her state of mind, but all the same — !" He made a small, disparaging grimace.

"I don't think she realizes how it sounds," said Eve. "Of course we have no idea what age she is."

"Young enough to enjoy self-pity, anyway!"

"There are self-pitying old maids and grandmothers, Tad."

"True."

"And she's not so much sorry for herself as bewildered and — up against it. Who is the man next door, do you think?"

"He'd better watch out, whoever he is!"

"I wish there was some way — " She picked up the letter and restored it to her hand-bag.

"Now, let it alone, Eve, for God's sake. Don't get mixed up in anything like that, you don't want any part of it!"

"I know." But her face was sad, reflective.

"Couple of psychopaths, probably," he warned her. "You could find yourself in real trouble. Don't answer her again."

"You couldn't just quietly find out who the man is — the one she's in love with?"

"Why?"

"There's something about those letters that you can't dismiss — however badly she's put it. I suppose you could call it almost a *cri du coeur*."

"Now, look, Evie, for the love of God, she's only some romantic crack-pot full of clichés and novel-reading — "

"You want to make something of that?" she flashed.

"What's the matter with novel-reading? We'd be in a pretty fix if people suddenly got too smart for novels!"

"Sure, so she's a good customer. But you don't have to do anything more for free. Write her a book, maybe. About fathers. But keep away from her in the meantime, because he's just the kind to try for libel."

"Everybody's got fathers," she reminded him.

"Everybody hasn't got Beaumont Marshall."

"I bet they call him Beau."

"Sure they do."

"Do you remember anything about his wife leaving him?"

"No. I can't keep track of all the wives in the neighborhood. It may have been twenty years ago."

"Who knows him? That you know."

"Oh, hell, Evie, you're not — "

"No, I suppose not, really. But finding her in your own back yard as it were — " She ran a perfect fingernail along the white cloth, thoughtfully. "I wonder if it *is* too late." And she lifted to him a long, clouded look which he held just for the pleasure of seeing her close like this, unaware of his scrutiny in her preoccupation. "She might still be young and attractive — to somebody, if not to this guy next door. She might still be able to build some sort of life if somebody — "

"If somebody interfered," he said. "Hunh-unh. Not you, anyway. I'm ag'in it."

"Tad. You did ask me to come up to your place for a weekend, didn't you."

"Hundreds of times, I should think. You always shy away as though I was making improper advances." Everyone knew that since the divorce his sister Frances had come to live in his Connecticut house and acted as hostess for him there.

"Now, Tad. You know I'm just not a good week-ender."

"Aren't you?" he asked with a sudden disarming wistfulness. "How would I know?" And then, seeing her still withdrawn and unsmiling, he added, "Shall I put a little cheese in the trap, then? I will ask the Selkirks in on Sunday for cocktails. And they, being advertising people, are at least on speaking terms with Marshall, or should be, because he works for them now and then."

"You mean, you'll give me a chance to pump them?" Bright eyes on his face now, parted lips, white teeth showing.

"You're awful cute," said Tad, and swallowed. "If that's the way to get my highly respectable week-end in the country with you, I'm too far gone to dicker."

"This is Tuesday," she announced, expectant.

"Yes, all right. On Friday I'll pick you up at your place about four o'clock and drive you out," he promised, against his better judgment.

iii

EVE decided it was better if Joanna didn't know that a personal encounter was even possible, and so delayed answering the second letter. During the intervening days till Friday she remembered the Marshalls at frequent intervals with a growing uneasiness, and once she nearly called the whole thing off — but that would have disappointed Tad, of whom she was very fond.

On Thursday she read the two letters again, aware of a fatalistic curiosity and compulsion — as though it was somehow inevitable that she was to become involved in what might prove to be an unhappy if not an unpleasant state of affairs. You'd think I was Dorothy Dix or somebody, with a mission to set everybody right on their private emotional idiocies, she would tell herself. If I do meet these people, and it's anything like she says, I'll never dare so much as mention a father in a book again, or they'll accuse me of using them as material. . . .

But still she did nothing to cancel the week-end, and that was her second mistake.

She stepped into Tad's car on Friday afternoon with somewhat the same sensations as she pursued the first elusive glimmer of each new story while it germinated in her brain — a mixture of curiosity, doubt, and hope. This one would never be written, of course. On paper, that is. But how if in some tactful, timely action or words she could re-write the rest of Joanna Marshall's life?

It was spring in Connecticut, she discovered as they drove. The Parkway was at the dogwood and early fruit blossom stage, and all the new little shades of green shimmered in the sunlight under a balmy wind. Tad said they had picked the right day, and let the car out discreetly. Eve said she forgot each winter how beautiful spring would be, and Tad, unusually owlish and understated because he was exceedingly happy, said that so, doubtless, had Persephone.

There was silence in the car, while both contemplated the legend of the kidnaped daughter of fertility.

"And yet, I sometimes wonder if finally she didn't get to feel rather cosy down there with Pluto, and wish that her mother had never interfered," Eve murmured, as though the matter had often occupied her thoughts, and Tad said, "One of the earliest mother-in-law stories must have arisen on that deal — perhaps the very first. Don't you wish you knew what it was?"

Eve laughed.

"Darling Tad, I do like you *so* much!"

"Well, good for me!" He spared her a glance from the road. "You couldn't put it a little stronger than that?"

"You're the most educated man I know," she hedged at once.

"Not much nourishment in that." The car let go another notch.

"But not what I say to all the boys," Eve assured him affectionately.

"It's not notably educated to have heard of Persephone," he complained, and she replied, "One shouldn't look a compliment in the teeth."

If you had asked Tad why he loved Eve Endicott so fatally, he might have said, Because of her mistakes. No one could make better mistakes more charmingly and innocently than she could, whether about her income tax, her television deals, or her impulsive efforts to work little miracles for her friends — what Tad called her me-fix complex. This Marshall campaign promised all sorts of complications, in which she would doubtless get her fingers pinched — it often came out that way — but Tad took up his usual first-aid post with his usual devoted resignation. You couldn't stop her from being good to people. You could only stand by. Sometimes it paid unexpected dividends, like this week-end visit he had been trying to wangle for months.

Tad's Connecticut house was a handsome grey stone and white clapboard place with big fireplaces and lots of windows — and it hardly deserved the drawling reference to a costly Hollywood set for a prosperous publisher's home which was Eve's only comment as she surveyed it with a smile from the gravel circle of the carriage-sweep in the trimmed green lawn.

Modest comfort, Tad insisted primly, lifting out her luggage. No butlers, observe. No flunkeys. Just a couple of nice old Irish biddies in the kitchen.

"Sure, sure, guests have to make their own beds and help with the washing up!" she nodded.

He gave her his gay, delighted grin around the horn-rim spectacles. She noticed again that he was very tall and well-knit, and he had nice teeth. What's the matter with me, Eve thought as she followed him up the steps. What am I waiting for, why don't I just give in and thank God?

Inside, the house was chintzy and book-ridden and friendly. Tad's sister Frances, herself many years a merry widow, was innocent of possessiveness or of apprehension that her place might some day be filled by a second wife. She liked living at Tad's, but she had enough money and friends of her own, and could just as well live somewhere else. At the moment, with an only son at Harvard, she found it convenient and cosy.

Her welcome to Eve Endicott was therefore without reservations, and her soft heart was wrung by Tad's somehow philosophical enslavement. He behaved, Fran thought, as though he had almost ceased to hope, and yet had no relish for a freedom which was useless to him. He was not a boy, and he did not parade his love for Eve. But seeing them together in his home, Fran was sure of what she had long suspected—Tad was not going to look at another woman for a long time to come.

She noticed too that Eve did not openly dangle him, though she must have known very well how he felt about her. Eve's tact and good manners were beyond reproach. They were both so damned civilized, Frances decided disgustedly, in the reflected light of her own hectic and enraptured courtship in a younger, more impulsive world. They wanted their heads knocked together. Tad's fault, of course. He should have sailed in more. Fran made a private resolve to be sufficiently uncivilized herself to advise him to pull up his socks and start pushing Eve around a little. They were neither of them getting any younger.

Bringing up the matter of his week-end a few days before, Tad had discovered to his surprise that while he was holed up in the study reading scripts his sister Fran had been getting round and about a bit. Fran knew all about the Marshalls. At least, she had encountered Beau two or three times at parties, and she had heard there was a daughter, who somehow never appeared. Certainly she had formed an impression of Beau. Not a nice man, Bell, she commented, quoting her favorite English detective character. Decorative enough, in an overstated sort of way, if you cared for that sort of thing. Told a good story, at too much length. Stayed reasonably sober. But not a nice man.

Well, said Tad, impressed, let's have a look at him, trot him out. Fran said she would try. But so far she had not, as you might say, cultivated Beau Marshall's acquaintance. He might turn her down. Tad said Have a go at getting the girl too. And Fran said she would try.

So the Selkirks came to cocktails on the Sunday, and Beau Marshall was with them. Quite a lot of miscellaneous other people were there also, and at first Eve had no opportunity to say more than "How-do-you-do" to him. The daughter, as usual, did not appear.

Eve was sitting on a sofa with a martini in her hand, beside a tall, dark, and noticeably un-handsome man with an old-fashioned in his, making small talk. She hadn't caught his name, and regretted it, for there had occurred between them that unforeseen, unpredictable spark which either happens at once or it doesn't, and which more often than not leads to something further, and in any case is never quite forgotten again.

His nose was too big, and his face was too long, and his mouth was rather heavy, and his eyes were slow and searching under black brows. His hair was straight and close-cut. His excellent clothes hung loosely on his bony, relaxed body. His voice undid one utterly. He kept it very low, perhaps deliberately intimate in the chatter-filled room. *Saturnine,* Eve thought, with a desperate clutch after indifference. I never saw that word walking round before — or sitting drinking an old-fashioned. Who owns this guy, I'm falling for it.

Casting about for something to take her mind off him, she decided to start her Marshall investigation right here. It didn't have to be the Selkirks. Everybody knew everybody at parties like this.

"Who is the man talking to the lady in the pink hat?" she asked, as if she didn't know.

"Beaumont Marshall." He left it at that.

"What does he do?"

"He's an artist of sorts. Does rather well with the cosmetic people — pretty girls in big hats and a roseleaf complexion — Use So-and-So's Face Powder."

"Is the pink hat his wife?"

"No. He hasn't got one."

"Is she yours, then?"

"My wife died last year," he said unemotionally.

"Oh — I'm sorry."

"It's all right. You must find it pretty confusing, to

be pitched into a mob like this. I know your name, but I bet you don't know mine."

"I'm afraid I don't," she admitted meekly.

"Richie Forrest. Eve Endicott. I may as well own up right now that I haven't read your books."

"I'm not surprised. Do you write or paint or what?"

"I just sit behind a desk down in Wall Street. I am fairly literate, in a general sort of way, but not so far as you are concerned. I shall take steps about that at once, of course."

"You wouldn't solemnly go out and buy my books on the strength of having had a drink with me here!" she laughed.

"Not if I didn't want to know more about you."

"Do you think that's any way to find out?"

"It's a beginning." His hooded, rather sleepy gaze rested on her unself-consciously.

Again she felt herself falling for it, and again retreated on to Beaumont Marshall.

"Does Mr. Marshall ever do illustrating?" she inquired — which had occurred to her as a basis for further acquaintance with Joanna's father if she needed to make use of it.

"Probably." He waited, relaxed, sardonic, attentive, for her next move.

"I just have a feeling I ought to know something about

him, and can't place it. He rings a bell somewhere," she said casually.

"Well, for God's sake," he remarked gently, "shall I go round him up so you can get the story of his life? It's not very pretty, but he'd probably be glad to fill it in for you."

She gave him an upward, enchanting look, chastened and ingratiating.

"I'd rather know about you," she said.

"So far it's been about six to one in favor of Marshall," he reminded her, without any special animus.

"Just talking," she said vaguely. There was a silence. "What's not pretty about him?" she asked then, and he made a move as though to carry out his threat of adding Marshall to their sofa for cross-questioning, so that she caught his sleeve with a gasp of laughter. "No, don't! I'm sorry. It's a defence mechanism. I don't dare ask questions about you, so I pick on him."

"You sure do," he agreed.

"And being a man, you don't gossip, and so the conversation dies. You don't talk about yourself either," she prodded after a moment.

"I'd love to, what shall I tell first? My golf score, my tailor, my bank references, my favorite flower, my telephone number—or what I dreamed about last night?"

"What did you dream about last night?" Their

eyes held, and the spark flashed between them again.

"I've forgotten now. Let's talk about you. Are you married, Eve Endicott?"

"I was. My husband died in the Bulge."

"That's tough, isn't it. I was there too. Only I was lucky."

"His name was Alan Fenwick. Captain."

Forrest shook his head.

"It was a small war sometimes. But I can't claim to have known him."

She liked him for not trying too hard.

"It was a long time ago," she reflected, and her life with Alan Fenwick seemed, looking back, as though it must have happened to some one else.

"It was, at that. I'm surprised you haven't been gathered in again before now by some character with brains in his head. Or is that a damn-fool kind of thing to say?"

"Writing books is a solitary job," said Eve. "I don't seem to get around much — like this, I mean."

"A likely story." He watched her a moment. "How do the words come? Much less the plots. I've often wondered. Maybe everybody asks authors that."

"It's hard to tell, usually, how it starts. I'm always suspicious of authors who can give elaborate descriptions of their mental processes. Perhaps I'm the one that's wrong, though — it's been suggested!"

"Well, here we are, now, sitting on a sofa talking. Would you write us like this?"

"Except that book dialogue is full of staircase wit — I'll think of much cleverer things to have said to you after it's too late. Writing gives you a chance to cross it out and try again."

"We could make a date," he suggested, "and you could say it then."

She considered him. Very quick on the uptake, wasn't he! Perhaps it had sounded as though she was hinting. His eyes were level and enigmatic, his heavy mouth was drawn into a small smile.

"You'd expect too much," she veered off in a queer panic.

"A nice quiet lunch," he persevered. "University Club? Thursday?"

"That would certainly be nice and quiet!" she was surprised into saying, and he in turn looked surprised at her reaction.

"The Louis XIV?" he offered then, as though searching his experience for liveliness. "Or is there some place you — "

"I'll settle for the club," she said hastily, and that was where she made another mistake.

"Good. One o'clock?"

She nodded, and asked, "*What* university?"

"Princeton."

"I might have known!"

"I'll take it as a compliment," he grinned.

"You may."

"Well, here comes your dream-boat. I'm glad I got that in when I did," he said, and glancing round she saw Beaumont Marshall on his way to their sofa, escorted by conscientious Tad.

"I'm very much interested in knowing you, Miss Endicott," Marshall began frankly, and his wide open blue eyes ran over her with a deliberate, conscious magnetism. "I hear a great deal about you. My daughter is a fan of yours — reads everything you write."

"Thank you," she said formally. "That's always nice to hear." She was aware of having a little lost sight of the original purpose of this party, which was to make discreet inquiries about the Marshalls and not sit about on sofas with tall dark strangers asking her to lunch. "Is your daughter here today?"

"Unfortunately for her, she isn't. She'll be very upset to have missed you." His smile at the prospect was broad and heartless, Eve thought.

"How old — " she was beginning, when Tad, having observed no greeting between the two men, inquired, "You know Richie Forrest, don't you, Marshall?"

"Hell, yes," said Joanna's father easily. "He's lived next door to us for years."

Eve saw that Tad heard it too, and had recognized

(though with a lesser shock) that here, as well as Joanna's father, was Joanna's outspoken idol next door.

"How old," she heard herself saying normally above a strange sensation in her midriff, "is your daughter, Mr. Marshall?"

"Twenty-two — twenty-three — she's always having birthdays." He shrugged them off with his effective, meaningless smile. Eve noticed that he filled his well-cut suit as it was meant to be worn, his groomed, receding hair had a discreet silvered wave, he gave out an impression of excessive cleanness, of a man just bathed and shaved and changed. A little too well turned out, like an actor who takes himself too seriously. She was sure without looking that his tie and handkerchief and socks were complementary. Beside him Tad and Richie Forrest looked as though they had slept in their clothes.

Forrest rose, murmuring something about a refill, and Tad went with him to the bar. Marshall took the place at Eve's side and continued to regard her with his wide, conquering blue stare.

"I must tell Joanna all about you," he said. "Let's see, now — young, beautiful, conservative, a little shy, navy blue and white — so *very* clever of you — " He inhaled ever so slightly. "Chanel Number Five out of a forty-dollar bottle — "

"She'll have an entirely false impression," Eve said

rather crossly, for though it was all true it sounded all wrong when he said it.

"Where did I miss?" he demanded, and she had no immediate answer.

"I think I had a letter from your daughter the other day," she ventured instead.

"Yes, I'm sure you did. In fact you've had two. I'm not supposed to know that, am I."

Her quick glance found his face guileless, almost expressionless, except for his habitual look of bland amusement. His eyes, so brilliantly blue, so round and open, were at the same time without depth, like polished windows with the blinds down behind them.

"She gets these crushes," he went on in his detached way, as though he was speaking of some one else's daughter, at least. "Once it was Fred Astaire, and she wanted to learn dancing — presumably with some idea of appearing as his partner. Once it was Barbara Stanwyck — because Stanwyck looked as though someone had kicked her in the teeth, Joanna said. Before that — oh, let's say Gary Cooper or Clark Gable. I'm thankful to note that it is not always a woman." He left a significant pause. "Joanna is a little — immature," he finished, with a distinct effect of understatement.

"Perhaps she doesn't get out enough — see enough people."

"Did she tell you so?"

She noticed that his lips were almost womanish, wide and clearly marked though not red, and that he could show his teeth on a brief question like that in a chilling way which was not a smile. She felt that she, and not Beaumont Marshall, was in the dock answering questions which might affect Joanna's life.

"In the letters? No." She spoke cautiously, anxious to betray nothing but the most casual interest, not at all in command of the conversation now. "She said something about envying the characters in my books."

"Well, who doesn't?" he asked pleasantly.

"You — you haven't read — ?" She wondered if her jaw had dropped.

"One or two. She leaves them about all over the house. I got curious. You're not at all what I would have expected, Miss Endicott."

"Well, what did you *think* I would be like?"

"From your books, a virginal, inexperienced nitwit like my daughter. But you've been around, Miss Endicott. How come you write these fairy tales?" He leaned towards her, his arm along the back of the sofa, his blue gaze knowing and confidential. "What are you hiding from?" he asked softly. "What are you so scared of?"

"I don't know what you mean," she said coolly, though it was a thing she never permitted anyone in her books to say. "I just happen to know nice people, and I prefer to write about that kind." Something about having no use for pathological cases which might have followed she bit off unsaid, under a renewed conviction that she was talking to one.

"Nice people," he repeated, and his eyes left her face to roam round the quietly convivial room. "Nice, respectable, God-fearing folk, eh? God bless us, every one." His teeth showed again on his words.

"Well, what kind of riff-raff are *you* accustomed to?" she demanded.

"This kind," he assured her cheerfully. "You like these people? You approve of them?"

"What I know of them, yes."

"Ah — what you know of them." He gave it great significance. "But what about the submerged seven-eighths?"

"You believe there is a skeleton in every cupboard, Mr. Marshall?"

"Well, isn't there?" He ran a derisive eye over the room again. "Take pretty Mrs. McKenzie in the pink flowered hat — there is a husband-secretary set-up there, which she very wisely chooses to ignore. Take our tall handsome host — when his wife departed for Reno, did he argue? No, of course not. He had irons in the fire. Take yours truly, sitting right here beside you — *my* wife was the type to leave a small child behind her when she lit out with another guy. Take Richie Forrest — he was all ready to take up with Joanna while he still wore a black band on his sleeve for a wife dead in childbirth — "

"*Really*, Mr. Marshall — !" She made an involuntary movement as though to rise.

"Oh, I put a stop to *that*," he assured her easily, without moving. "You should see my heavy-father act, Miss Endicott, it's a dilly." His challenging gaze held hers again, until it seemed that he had read her mind and was aware that she had entertained ideas of acting on behalf of his daughter who was after all perhaps not quite all there — as though he tacitly acknowledged as an unfortunate necessity the very sort of thing Joanna had written about him.

"I think I should like to meet your daughter," she said, in defiance of her own qualms.

"I doubt it. She's a very commonplace young woman. Pretty, of course, like her mother. I have done my best to cope with the — hereditary taint, not very successfully, I'm afraid."

"Perhaps you would bring her to tea some afternoon. At my apartment in New York."

"Why?" he inquired, smiling.

"I'm — always interested in young people trying to find themselves."

"No interest whatever in her old man?"

She wondered if he actually believed that she was using Joanna as a bridge to further acquaintance with his fascinating self, and decided that if the man's cast-iron egotism was the only approach, she must make use of it, to break down what was rapidly becoming a rather sinister mystery — two people living together in what sort of daily climate, each implying to the most casually encountered stranger that the other was off his rocker. Which one of the Marshalls was the mad one? Eve knew that it was too late now to remind herself that it was none of her business. She was being drawn, step by step, into their lives.

"Do you ever do any illustrating?" she asked impersonally. "For the fiction magazines, I mean. It's so hard to get an artist to even *read* your story — if you mention that your heroine has short red hair she's likely to come out in the pictures with a taffy-colored mane."

"It's a field I'd like to get into," he replied. "Got anything coming up?"

"Yes, I have. Nothing guaranteed, of course, so far."

"If I promise to draw the right kind of hair, will you give me a chance at the art editor?"

"It depends on the magazine, you know. I have no authority."

"Naturally."

"It's an idea." She appeared to turn it over in her mind. If the worst came to the worst, she could always get Keating on the *Metropolitan* to play along with her scheme. "I raised cain about the illustrations for my last one."

"Maybe we should get together on it," he murmured.

"Maybe."

Their eyes met, wary, half-antagonistic, half-friendly. Already they were opponents in some still unspecified game. She was surprised that he had taken her up so quickly. Not just because he was interested in her as a woman, she felt sure. Perhaps merely the acquisitive part of him, after an illustrating job. Perhaps—well, what, to keep an eye on her interest in Joanna?

"Then do come to tea," she suggested again. "I could let you have a carbon of the script any time now. You can mull it over and see if it appeals to you. Say Tuesday or Wednesday of this week?" Thursday was Richie Forrest. She wanted to see Joanna before lunching with Richie Forrest.

"Wednesday, then," he agreed.

"About four. I'll give you the address."

"Joanna has the address—remember?"

"And bring Joanna with you, please." It amounted to a condition, and he shrugged resignedly.

"If you insist."

"I'd like to see her."

"There is just one thing, Miss Endicott," he said levelly. "People sometimes have a tendency to try to draw Joanna out, I think is the expression—that is, to enlarge her ego, and encourage her, shall we say, obsessions. And while it may be meant for the best, I assure you that I regard it as pure interference in a private matter which I prefer to deal with in my own way."

She stared at him.

"B-but surely she — "

He rose and stood looking down at her with what seemed like open satisfaction at her bewilderment.

"May I get you a drink?" he said, holding out his hand for the empty glass in hers. "Martini, wasn't it? Same as me."

She surrendered the glass and rose also, drifting beside him towards the bar, where Tad was. She felt a sudden need for Tad's very sane proximity. She was both shaken and enraged by Beaumont Marshall's readiness to slay in a few cool, well-chosen words the reputation and privacy of anyone on whom his shallow blue glance lighted. And moreover, she suspected from the look which accompanied his remark about Tad's other irons in the fire that it was aimed at herself.

iv

CONTEMPLATING the past week-end in cold blood on Monday morning at her apartment, Eve came to the reluctant conclusion that she had somehow jockeyed herself into putting the cart before the horse. She had allowed it to matter to her how she stood with regard to Richie Forrest, instead of concentrating on Joanna. She was afraid to lunch with him until she had seen the girl, because she knew that from now on her attitude towards him must depend on the sort of person Joanna proved to be. And yet, had she put the Marshall case first, she would have done it the other way round and taken the opportunity during the meal of getting his opinion of Joanna's letters and the situation she herself had created.

On Wednesday she laid her prettiest tea-table and a lavish spread of sandwiches and sweets, as though preparing a party for a child, and she took pains with her own appearance. Promptly at four the colored maid opened the door to them, and Joanna entered the room at her father's side.

She was lovely.

That was all Eve took in at first. Joanna Marshall was fair and slight and dressed like a schoolgirl, with a round, brimmed hat like a halo on her soft, shoulder-length hair. She stood rooted while her father said non-committally, "This is my daughter Joanna, Miss Endicott." Her hand was small and fleeting in Eve's, and her response to Eve's greeting was inaudible. Clutched to her side, she carried a copy of Eve's newest book, for autographing.

Seated on the sofa beside the tea-table, Joanna remained tense and speechless, while her father made conversation with their hostess. For a while Eve ignored her tactfully (the dog and baby technique) but when the tea was poured and sufficient time had elapsed she remarked directly to the girl, "Wasn't it odd, my running into your father like that, so soon after getting your letter?"

Joanna swallowed visibly and said, "It was like a book."

"Yes, it was, rather," Eve agreed shamelessly, and then to cover her own guilty tracks without regard to the facts, she went on — "It only goes to prove what I always say — no author would dare allow himself the coincidences that happen every day in his own life."

"Oh, I do realize that," Joanna replied humbly. "And I realize that I shouldn't have said what I did about the ending of your book, I — "

"But you were quite justified in that," Eve insisted hastily, for she had intended no rebuke. "Except that prayers are answered, and situations do ravel themselves out even more unexpectedly in life than they do in books."

"Yes, I — suppose they do, with luck," Joanna submitted, and Eve saw with distress that she had taken it to heart. Joanna's hands holding her cup were not quite steady, and it seemed she was afraid to drink her tea for fear of spilling it.

Eve rose and moved a small table close to Joanna's knees.

"Put your cup down there," she suggested, "and you'll have a free hand for a sandwich."

"Thank you," Joanna whispered. The hand which came up to the sandwich tray Eve held out to her was so fragile as to look almost transparent.

"And just what was it you shouldn't have said about the ending of Miss Endicott's book?" her father inquired in icy patronizing tones.

Joanna kept her eyes down, away from his face.

"I — only said — "

"It was only a question of the happy ending," Eve

cut in mercifully. "As you already know, Mr. Marshall, I refuse to admit that the only realistic way to finish a book is with everybody dead or dying or divorcing. Boy does get girl, every day in the week."

"Was my daughter skeptical of that?" he asked, in a bearing-down sort of way.

"Oh, no, I — " Joanna flashed a look of appeal at Eve and tried to raise her cup, with a hand that shook all the way.

"I believe it's you who are the skeptic, Mr. Marshall," Eve said, in another attempt to divert his attention from Joanna.

"I don't presume, however, to write letters to successful authors giving unsolicited advice," he observed, and his eyes remained on Joanna's face as though he willed her to meet his gaze, until to Eve's dismay she did so, with the immobile, trapped obedience of the rabbit with the snake. "I think perhaps you owe Miss Endicott an apology," he suggested.

"I — I said just now that I shouldn't have said it — " Joanna's face was white and her lips trembled.

"I don't think that will quite do," he replied, with an effect of reluctant reproof. "I think you should say, 'It was very stupid of me to criticize your work, Miss Endicott.' "

"It was very s-st — " Joanna began, and at a little gesture from him she turned her head so that she faced Eve at the tea-table and began again. "It was very st-stupid of me — "

"Oh, nonsense," Eve broke in lightly, herself emerging from a kind of paralysis, "you're making too much of a simple remark — "

"Kindly allow her to finish," said Marshall, sitting motionless, his eyes on the girl, who sat equally still, facing Eve, whose turn it was now to stammer.

"Well, I'm s-sorry, but I — "

"Now, Joanna."

"It was very stupid of me to criticize your work, Miss Endicott," she recited softly into the silence.

"Thank you, Joanna, it was quite unnecessary to apologize," Eve replied with all the warmth and sympathy she could get into the words, feeling she must use all her wits to win Joanna's confidence and overcome her humiliation. "Your father and I are doing a dicker about illustrating my new script for a magazine," she went on almost at random. "I have promised to let him take a copy to look through, so you'll have a chance to read it before publication if you like."

"Yes, I'd — love to — when he has finished with it. It's always hard to wait for the next one."

"Be careful, Miss Endicott. She'll be telling you how to make it more realistic," said Marshall.

"Now, I do think that's enough of that," Eve observed reasonably.

"She's a great authority on life, you know." He overrode her protest with apparent amiability, so that she wondered if he was after all just a heavy-handed tease or if it was bear-baiting at its worst. In either case something ought to be done to get Joanna out of his influence, such treatment was barbarous to a sensitive girl. Any sort of excuse must be found to see her again, anything that would not look to him like the interference he objected to. "Between novels like yours and Hollywood films," he was saying, "she knows all the answers. And now she's asking for television to broaden her outlook still further."

"I know it's fashionable to look down one's nose at television," Eve took him up with some spirit. "But it's very much worth having in the house, all the same."

"Potted Shakespeare," he suggested as a polite concession. "She wouldn't look at that. She'd go for the love stories."

"I don't go for potted Shakespeare myself," Eve retorted smoothly. "May I fill your cup, Mr. Marshall? Joanna, try one of these cakes, there's a little French bakery round the corner that makes a specialty of them."

Joanna shook her head with the glazed and cautious look of one who knows that the first blink will cause tears to run down her face. She had not touched a mouthful since that first shaky sip of tea.

"Don't sulk, Joanna," said her father's silky voice.

"Miss Endicott has gone to some trouble. Take one of the cakes and eat it."

Joanna took a cake and bit into it. As she did so, the brimming tears spilled over and her cheeks were wet. Eve set down the plate with a little smack.

"Mr. Marshall, I hate scenes, and I don't often speak my mind like this," she said, determinedly pleasant. "But I think the time has come for me to say that you are behaving abominably."

"I warned you, Miss Endicott," he reminded her in a playful singsong.

"Why?" said Eve, holding on to herself. "Tell me why you choose to, shall we say, tease Joanna unmercifully before a stranger. It's not kind. It's not funny. I don't see the point."

"There's no need for you to see the point. That's between Joanna and me. As I told you before we came here."

"I shouldn't have come!" cried Joanna, startling them both. "That's what I ought to apologize for, Miss Endicott! It's so often like this, I knew what I might be letting you in for! It's not fair to you, when he goes on like this. But I wanted to come here — I thought perhaps this time — " She stood up, and by a visible effort gained control of herself. "Please forgive me. Can we go now, Father?"

"What about your book?" he asked as he rose, unruffled, at his leisure. "You were going to ask Miss Endicott to write in it, weren't you?"

"It doesn't matter." Joanna glanced back at the sofa where the copy of Eve's novel lay forgotten, and took a step towards the door.

"I'd be glad to," Eve said quickly, and picked up the book. "Let me get a pen."

She carried the book with her into the study where she worked, and inscribed the flyleaf. Then on a scratch-pad she wrote her telephone number and added below it: *Ring up and come have lunch with me.* Feeling a little melodramatic, she slipped the small paper between the middle pages of the book, which she returned to Joanna in the other room. Then she lifted the copy of the script from the table where she had laid it ready, and said to Marshall, "Are you really interested in illustrating this thing on spec?"

"Yes, indeed," he replied, taking it from her. "Especially now." And he gave her his blank, significant smile.

She surrendered it to him, knowing that it was the best excuse for another meeting with the Marshalls. Somebody would have to get her out of the deal later on if it wouldn't do. The main thing now was to maintain some kind of contact, if only the right to request the return of the script.

But even as the bulky envelope changed hands she had a sharp moment of misgiving. So easy to have forgotten it, or made some delay, and eased them out of her door forever. They were at best uncomfortable companions, and no telling what they might amount to at worst. She knew what Tad would say. But first she would find out what Richie Forrest said.

Marshall had paused to look over Joanna's shoulder as she stood reading the inscription in the book: *For Joanna Marshall, with affectionate regards,* EVE ENDICOTT. Nothing wrong with that. Then, while they both watched him helplessly, he caught the projecting corner of the scratchpad paper between his finger and thumb and drew it out of the book and read it, beyond Joanna's reach. Eve felt her cheeks get hot, like a schoolgirl caught in a scrape. He crushed the paper in his hand and tossed it contemptuously on to the tea-table.

"That is the kind of thing I don't tolerate, Miss Endicott," he said quietly. "Good afternoon."

Joanna looked back at Eve as he opened the door, and then preceded him through it. Eve stood staring at the wooden panels. It seemed to her that there was sheer fright on Joanna's face, and she was uneasily aware that with the best intentions in the world she had probably only made things worse.

V

SO the seesaw had swung again, and now the most important thing about the lunch with Richie Forrest was the light he could shed on Joanna Marshall. Eve knew now who owned the guy who had struck sparks at Tad's on Sunday — or should in the natural course of events acquire him. Joanna was young — she needed help — she was in love with him. It made sense. What was he doing about it? A recent widower, obviously nothing much. How much was he prepared to do if nothing — if nobody interfered?

She took Joanna's first letter with her to the University Club. The second, with its embarrassing frankness about the man next door, she decided to mislay. Since yesterday afternoon she was able to write off as naiveté the apparent bad taste of Joanna's revelations. Joanna was, as her father had suggested, immature — and furthermore, she was dying of loneliness. *Cri du coeur* was in this case hardly Gallic exaggeration.

When the cocktails had come and the order had been given, Eve looked at Richie Forrest across the table with a small fatalistic sigh. He was good, he was sweet, he was a great guy. And he was interested. If it wasn't for Joanna — Yet, if it wasn't for Joanna they would never have met anyhow. The only thing to do now was to go along with it, and see how it came out. Maybe, if they succeeded in rescuing Joanna something would turn up. Meanwhile, sit tight. Watch it. No stars in the eyes. Plenty of time for that later.

They touched glasses.

"First of all," said Eve, "I have a confession to make."

He wasn't a wise-cracker. If he had nothing to say, he said it, in attentive silence.

She laid Joanna's letter on the table between them. He didn't seem to recognize the handwriting, but you couldn't be sure.

"I'd like you to read it," she said. "Please understand, that sort of thing is very common in my mail. I get a lot of touching, confidential stuff. But this one — well, read it."

He left his cocktail standing and read the letter without comment, till he had finished. His face was brooding and sad.

"Poor kid," was all he said, as he laid it down on the cloth again.

"You know all about them, I suppose. You are the man next door, aren't you?"

"Yep." He was twirling his cocktail glass slowly, his eyes on the amber contents.

"Are you — is anyone doing anything about it?"

He looked up at her, with apparent reluctance to meet her eyes.

"What would you suggest?" he asked, without irony.

"Mr. Forrest, *I* want to do something. That was the reason I asked all those questions about Beaumont Marshall last Sunday at Tad's. In fact, I got Tad to arrange that party so that I could ask questions. I didn't know that you would materialize there too. Nor I didn't know that Marshall himself would turn up in person. It was the Selkirks we were aiming at."

He nodded, turning his glass.

"You wouldn't talk about him then," she said, with some exasperation. "You won't talk now. Why? What's holding you back? I suppose you know he's got his knife into you."

"I know. That makes me pretty useless as a go-between."

"I'm not asking you to be a go-between. I'm only asking you to fill in the thing for me. You've known about this situation for years, apparently. I've only just started.

How did it get this way? What goes on? I've seen them together now, he brought her to tea at my apartment."

He gave her a quick, surprised look.

"How did you manage that?"

"I offered him a possible illustrating job as bait — asked him to pick up a script to read — asked him to bring her along. He already knew that she had written me. He seems to know everything she does. He warned me off. But he brought her."

"You seem to have made more progress than anyone else can."

"Have you tried?" she demanded.

"My wife tried." There was a long silence, while she waited for him to go on. "She was always trying. She'd ask them to dinner, and she'd ask Joanna to have tea with her alone."

"Did they come to dinner?"

"Oh, yes. But it was seldom very successful, and we used to doubt if it was any real kindness to Joanna."

"Why wasn't it a success?"

"He loves to torment her before people. If we could get Joanna to say anything, which wasn't easy, he was likely to ridicule or contradict her, or wind her all up in what had begun as just a casual remark. I've seen her in tears, and I've felt myself sweating, before he let her go."

"That's what happened yesterday. One can't seem to get her off the hook."

"Naturally you can't inflict that sort of thing on just any ordinary dinner party. A few of us used to brace ourselves every so often and have another try, and sometimes we'd get away with it. Margie had a knack of heading him off, but since she died he's made several very trying scenes and I think people have pretty well given up inviting them anywhere together. It's not worth it."

"Well, are you all going to just sit back and *leave* it at that?"

"What can we do, Miss Endicott? The man's not certifiable. He doesn't beat her or starve her. She's not a child, she's come of age."

"Yes, I know, but — " Eve drank off the rest of her cocktail and refused a second, as the food arrived. "Did you know her mother too? What happened there?"

"It happened just after we moved into the neighborhood. We had only seen them a few times — dinners, tennis, cocktails, and so on. We weren't aware that there was any serious trouble between them. At that time he seemed to be only a rather sarcastic, egotistical character who fancied himself as a lady-killer in a harmless kind of way."

"And the mother?"

"Very much like Joanna is now, but not so much under his thumb."

"Well, what happened? What sort of man did she run away with?"

"I don't expect you to believe this, but he was the chauffeur. We still had chauffeurs in those days. And believe it or not, I honestly don't know what the fellow looked like, though I must have seen him around. We supposed he was kind to her. We supposed there must have been some kind of row with Marshall and she simply took off with this guy on an unfortunate impulse. And we guessed she would hardly have dared to come back, even if she had wanted to."

"You mean sympathy at the time was with her — even though she left a child behind, with a man like that?"

"Joanna was supposed to worship her father then. I don't know that there was much actual sympathy for Mrs. Marshall, but we did think it must have been some unexpected crisis which drove her away."

"Such as Marshall caught the chauffeur kissing his wife?"

"Maybe. It wouldn't have gone much farther than that, I'd say, judging by what we'd seen of her. On the other hand, it might have been carefully planned as an elopement, I don't suppose we'll ever know now."

"How long since she went away?"

"Must be fifteen years."

"Doesn't anyone know what's become of her?"

"I doubt it. Marshall wouldn't give her a divorce, so it can't be much of a life for her, she couldn't marry. That's his revenge, I suppose."

"Part of it," said Eve. "He's taking the rest of it out on Joanna. Would it be because of the resemblance to her mother that he treats her the way he does?"

"Could be. Mostly, I think he's simply got more and more bitter and vicious over his own humiliation. It must be quite a shock to an egotist like that to have a woman walk out on him publicly — so he strikes out at anything he can hurt in return."

"Which happens to be his daughter."

"You know, if she'd stand up to him and fight back he'd have more respect for her. If anyone in this world could handle him it was Margie, for the simple reason that she wouldn't take any lip from him. Margie had red hair, and she never hesitated to tell him off till *I* felt like taking cover. But he seemed to enjoy it. If he cared about anybody he cared about Margie. He sat there at the funeral with tears running down his face. Somebody like Margie might have tamed him, if he'd married that kind — made him toe the line. Joanna asks for trouble — brings out all the worst in him."

"But Margie couldn't save Joanna from him."

"No. Not that she wouldn't have gone on trying. When Joanna was a child it wasn't so bad, she was in and out of our house all the time. Margie had lost one baby, and the second one killed her. But she wanted children, and she adored Joanna. We even used to dream of adopting her. That was crazy, of course. The older Joanna got the more difficult it was to get her away from him, even for an afternoon. He made her model for him — that kept her under his eye. She's never had friends of her own age, never been to kid parties or dances with the young set. It drove Margie wild, but he wouldn't listen, even to her. Joanna has grown up a pitiful bundle of nerves and complexes — but what can you do?"

"I'm going to do *something*, Mr. Forrest. And you're going to help me."

He shook his head ruefully.

"Don't count much on me. My name is mud with Beau, I haven't been inside their house for months."

"Don't you *care?*" she asked desperately, and he laid down his fork.

"Look, Miss Endicott, Joanna is a sweet kid, and I'd like to see her live a nice, normal life. But for years I watched my wife run her head into a stone wall on this thing, and she got nowhere. You can't expect me to enjoy the same prospect for you."

"Why is he so down on you?"

"How did you know he was?"

"He passed a remark on Sunday."

"I'll bet he did. Got a tongue like an adder."

"He objects to your taking an interest in Joanna — so soon after your wife's death."

"Oh, that." He nodded grimly. "I was driving back

from the station one afternoon, and I saw Joanna walking along the street alone, crying. I stopped the car and got her into it and drove around a little while. She was almost hysterical and not very coherent about what had happened at home — I gathered it was just one of his bad days, when he made her pose for him and then nagged her all the time. Finally when she had got hold of herself a bit I left the car in front of my house and took her inside and gave her a glass of sherry. It was the sort of thing I would have done if Margie had been there. I didn't think anything about it, I'm not used to it yet that Margie isn't there any more. God knows I had no designs on the girl. Marshall saw us go in, waited about ten minutes and then came after her. He was as unpleasant as possible, but I don't think she understood much of what he meant to imply. Of course it was perfectly ridiculous, there was no secrecy about her being there, and the meeting hadn't been planned."

There was a long, thoughtful silence. The second letter lay heavy on Eve's mind. He had not spoken of Joanna like a man who suspected that she was in love with him — as Joanna imagined that he did — or like a man who was at all in a frame of mind to console himself for the death of his wife. She wondered what would happen if it were suggested to him that Joanna was devoted to him, not just as the child he seemed to consider her. It might rouse him to more effort on her behalf, or, still grieving for Margie, he might recoil from the idea as an awkward complication. Eve decided it wasn't time yet, at least, to make any mention of Joanna's second letter with its open declaration — and then wondered if she was holding it back because of her own sudden feeling for Richie Forrest or strictly in Joanna's interest. His quiet simplicity and obliging concentration on a subject which he had certainly not expected to discuss at this meal turned Eve's heart over again.

"There's one thing more," she said slowly. "I'm afraid I made a gaffe yesterday afternoon."

He gave her an inquiring look over his plate, but said nothing. She had never known anyone so unconcerned about silences.

"I was horrified at his behavior," she went on unwillingly. "And I tried to give her my telephone number, so that we might have lunch together — without him listening in, I thought. I had some idea of helping her to — well, get away from him now and then, at least, and enjoy herself on her own. He caught me. He noticed the paper and read it and destroyed it right in front of me. And now of course he's furious with me, and will probably keep me at arm's length."

"You shouldn't have done that," he said mildly, eating his lunch.

"Yes, I know that now!" she cried impatiently. "Say something constructive, can't you?"

He looked at her across the table with a slow, affectionate smile.

"You always lead with your heart, don't you," he said.

"Maybe I do. You'd think I'd know better, at my age."

"I hope you never learn. There aren't too many like that around these days."

"But it didn't help Joanna. She looked scared to death when they left."

"That's nothing new."

"How can you just *sit* there — !"

"I've told you before, the last time I tried to help her I put my foot in it," he reminded her patiently. "If you can come up with one practical suggestion — "

"All right. You could marry her." She had not meant to say it.

It caught him totally off guard, in the act of cutting a piece of steak. For the fraction of a second his hands were still, as though a deep, paralyzing pain had shot through him. Then he laid down his knife and fork, carefully parallel as though he had finished his meal, and at last met her eyes.

"You talk too much," he said quietly.

"Well, it — I was only — "

"Guessing?" He did not smile.

"What kind of a guy *are* you? You could be in love with her — and yet here you are, sitting on your hands!"

"Now, wait a minute," he cautioned, in that almost inaudible voice. "Don't go off at me like that. Such a thing never occurred to me — naturally — until very recently, and I still have no idea what it's worth. I don't want you to get any wrong ideas. She was just the kid next door, you know — and my marriage to Margie was something pretty special. When I lost her, I didn't see how life was going to amount to much, from there on in. The thought of — well, of falling in love again, whether with anyone we'd known, or with a stranger — beginning again, with anybody else — I didn't want any part of it. I felt I'd had the best, and I don't like imitations."

"I know all about that," she nodded sympathetically. "And yet they keep reminding you how many years you've still got to live, and how dreary it is to grow old all alone — "

"Yes, you get a lot of good advice," he sighed. "All for your own good, and of course all disinterested, as you've doubtless noticed too."

"I've had time for a lot more of that than you have," she agreed with a grin. "None of it took, though. But now you've had a glimmer?"

"It was that day I took her home with me. Well, I don't have to dot the i's for you — you're way ahead of me, aren't you. Remember, the house is just as Margie left it — except for the emptiness. And I was used to seeing Joanna in it, there was nothing new about that. In those few minutes before Marshall came barging in — I wasn't alone."

"Yes, I see," Eve said gently. "And yet she wasn't a usurper."

"That was it, I think. She sort of belonged there. She sat on the end of the sofa where she'd sat hundreds of times before, with that sherry glass in her hand — feeling comforted and safe, as I'd seen her with Margie in the room. It was almost as though nothing had happened — to Margie. It felt like home again."

Eve reached out and touched his sleeve briefly.

"Then get on with it," she said. "It's the right thing for both of you."

But his eyes followed her hand in its retreat.

"I'm not sure that it is," he said thoughtfully. "She's only a kid. She doesn't know beans. I feel more like a father to her, after all. And how come I talk to you like this, the second time I see you? It's witchcraft."

"It's Joanna," she told him, deliberately matter-of-fact. "She needs us. Can't afford to fool around."

He sat looking at her a moment, amused and kind.

"You're the sort of girl to give the shirt off your back, aren't you," he murmured then.

"Oh, nonsense," she said briskly. "I just like to see happy endings."

"Why don't you get around to write yourself one?"

"Well, I — I will, one of these days. How do you know I haven't?"

"I hope you have. I hope it's the good guy I think it is."

She didn't have to let him go on thinking it was Tad, she told herself without replying to him. She didn't have to bow out so gracefully and so soon, in Joanna's favor. He wasn't really spoken for yet. He hadn't made up his mind to anything — yet. There were several kinds of witchcraft . . .

"I've been catching up on my reading," he remarked after a minute, bringing things round to the more personal plane which he had intended for today.

vi

ONE of the main hazards of living with Beaumont Marshall, as even his servants could testify, was that he had good-humored days. And when that started, you forgot the rest of it, you levelled off with him, you were flattered and grateful, you lowered your guard, and usually you let yourself in for something. But such was his charm at such times, and his expansive blue-eyed bonhomie, that you never learned.

Breakfast in the sunny dining-room of his brick house in the fashionable Connecticut suburb had been a ritual ever since the day that ten-year-old Joanna, feeling important and grown up, had taken over her mother's deserted chair at the end of the table behind the silver coffee service, and presided with gravity and grace over her father's morning meal. And often at breakfast time before the irritations of daily living got at him, he was at his best, and Joanna's day would begin hopefully. He seldom cherished a mood overnight. He preferred to build them up fresh every day. To take advantage of the peaceful interludes, it was necessary to cultivate a short memory and let yesterday's bygones be bygones, so that Joanna always came down to breakfast as it were on tiptoe in the effort to preserve the overnight calm as long as possible.

She was not surprised, therefore, to find him seated at the table smiling and serene, looking through his morning mail, on the day after the visit to Eve's apartment. She kissed his cheek as usual, and sat down behind the coffee urn and handed him his cup prepared as he liked it. She was wearing a pink dress, and her pale hair gleamed with brushing and swung childishly against her cheeks as she turned her head. The sun sparkled across silver and china, and the cheerful fragrance of bacon and coffee was in the room. Marshall surveyed her with approval, as she buttered a piece of toast and reached for the jam.

"In the pink this morning, eh?" he remarked shamelessly, and waited for her responsive giggle. "You look fine, Totsy, really fine. What's on for today?"

It was always a good sign when he called her Totsy — a little name left over from the days when they were always good friends. After there had been a row and her mother had retired behind a locked door, he would turn for company to the child and amuse himself by demonstrating what good companions they were, and how easy it was to get along with him if one was only willing to try. And the young Joanna, bewildered by her mother's behavior, would respond to him gratefully, trusting and flattered, seeing only his charm, his playfulness, his subtle bribery and deliberate fascination.

"I thought I'd run down to the library and change our books," she said. "Anything special you want?"

He appeared to weigh the matter seriously.

"Well, maybe a nice detective story."

"Yes, naturally!" she laughed. "That is, I'll bring you one, and hope it's nice. I meant anything else."

"Still waiting for Churchill's new one. Suppose we ought to buy that, for the shelves."

"You bought the last one, I know."

"All right. Go into the shop and charge it, and bring it back with you."

"Will you be working this morning?" she asked, always ready to be friendly and interested in his doings when she got an opening. "Or did you finish it?"

"Finish what? Oh, the soap ad. Not quite. I'm going to work, all righty, but on something else." He paused mysteriously. "I'm going to lay out something for Miss Endicott's new story."

"Did you read it last night?" She would not have dared to bring it up herself, but he was smiling. "What's it about? Did you like it? May I have it now? What's it called?"

"You know what, Totsy? She's an amazing woman. She *believes* that stuff."

"So do I," declared Joanna, risking disaster.

"That's *not* surprising." But there was no sting in the words. "She's older than you are — had more experience. Had a husband once, killed in the war. Can't think what she's been up to ever since then. She reminds me of someone."

"I know," Joanna agreed gently.

"You noticed it too?"

"I don't — " Joanna became cautious. "I'm not sure I know what you mean."

"You know perfectly well what I mean. She reminds you of someone too, doesn't she." He waited, and then said it himself, not looking at her. "She reminds you of Margie Forrest."

"Well, yes, I — did think of it yesterday. It's not so much her looks, it's just — well, something about her."

"Something about her." He mused a moment, his eyes on the coffee urn, and Joanna stole a look at his face. His grief over Margie Forrest's death had turned him savage and unapproachable for days, and she had seen him weeping at the funeral.

"I wonder if Richie noticed it too," she ventured.

"We start even this time," he said quietly to the coffee urn, and then before her astonishment could become visible on her expressive face he went on lightly, as though the words had not been uttered, "Do you think we could manage a week-end visitor with only Mrs. Thing to help, or should we try to get somebody to live in?"

Joanna gaped at him silently.

"Your front teeth will fall out," he advised her politely, "if you don't pull up your jaw."

"You mean — ask Miss Endicott *here?*" she gasped.

"Well, why not?" He was excessively reasonable, but with a reckless glint in his eyes. "You like her. I like her. Of course if it's too much trouble to have a visitor — "

"Oh, *no*, I'd love to — if you think she'll come — "

The jovialness left him abruptly.

"And why do you think she wouldn't?" It was an open challenge to her to refer to his badgering behavior the day before, and Miss Endicott's sharp reaction to it.

"I d-didn't mean — that is, we don't know her very well."

"Business proposition," he asserted, with a phony gravity not intended to ring true.

"You mean I can write and ask — "

"*I* shall write this time," he said pleasantly. "Makes it more official, what?"

"Father, I don't see — " Suspicion closed in on her delight. Doubt. Foreboding. There must be something behind all this. He was usually up to something when he seemed most aboveboard and innocent. And yet — that reference to Margie Forrest. The only real part of him, the part you could get along with, the part you could love, had belonged to Margie Forrest, who was happily married and didn't want it. He was much worse since she died. If Eve Endicott could in some way fill Margie's place in his life — make it up to him, somehow, for losing the only human being who had ever really mattered to him —

"Well, what's so strange about it?" he demanded wilfully, but without bad temper, without bearing down. "She came to Tad Benson's for a week-end. We'll get some of the same crowd here on the Sunday. Been quite a while since we've thrown a party. Think you can manage it?"

"Well, I'll — try."

"Good for you. Nobody can do more."

She sat staring at him, still incredulous, as he returned airily to his letters. This was the way he used to be — when you almost dared to trust him — when sometimes you could go for days without a scene. All because of Eve Endicott? And in spite of yesterday afternoon? Not a word had passed between them that she hadn't overheard. Since then he had read the new script. . . .

DEAR MISS ENDICOTT [*Joanna wrote, sitting at a table in the village library later that day*] —

Something very strange has happened. My father is writing to ask you to come here for a week-end visit. He is taking it for granted that he will get the job of illustrating your script and I do hope nothing goes wrong about that, he will be so disappointed and angry.

But please, Miss Endicott, could you come anyway? Because it has made such a difference in him since he started to think about it. I know he behaved very badly yesterday, and I allowed it to upset me because I so wanted to be *your* kind of people and not have a scene. But you see, with him these things pass over and are forgotten, and he expects you to do the same. He was quite *gay* at breakfast today, and he even gave me money for extras without being asked, and when I left the house to do some errands he kissed me good-bye, the way he used to.

Miss Endicott, I think you have worked some kind of miracle. He read your new script last night, could that have anything to do with it? Of course he has good days, and it doesn't last — but I always hope it will.

I am writing this because no one could expect you — no one but him — could expect you to risk another performance like yesterday, but I wanted to say that he needn't be like that if he chooses — and because I would so love to have you come, and will do my best to avoid anything like a scene while you are here.

Sincerely,
JOANNA MARSHALL

DEAR MISS ENDICOTT [*wrote Beaumont Marshall by the same mail*] —

I sat up most of the night reading your blasted, beautiful script, trying to sell myself the idea that it was just ivory-tower stuff and all done with mirrors, but that won't work any more. You have got me wondering, Miss Endicott, and that's bad.

I woke this morning with a double-page layout for the picture complete in four colors in my head — and if nobody ever sees it but you and me I shall still have to commit it to paper to get rid of it now. Perhaps you would follow up your suggestion that Joanna is too much alone by breaking our monotony here with a week-end visit. Would next Friday suit you? I shall be lunching in town and could drive you back here with me in the afternoon.

Yours,
BEAU MARSHALL

With the two letters on the desk in front of her, Eve stifled the usual impulse to consult Tad. Tad would be against it, she didn't have to ask to be sure of that. Richie Forrest was the one to inform of this latest move in the game, because she meant to accept, and it was only fair to warn him what was afoot. Besides, she wanted him on her team.

She found him in the telephone directory and gave her name to a secretary and he came on the wire without delay.

"Good morning," he said cordially, and waited. She had never known a man with so few extra words.

She explained about her mail, and read him Marshall's note and said How about that, anyway?

"Started something, didn't you," he said then.

"Well, yes, but what? He doesn't need work all that

bad, does he? I mean, I can't put his illustration through, no matter how much I like it, he must know that."

"No, he doesn't need the work."

"Well, *what?* Got any ideas?"

"Several. Are you sure you want to go on with this?"

"Sure I'm sure! How else can I get at Joanna, other than string along with this illustrating idea at least till it trips me up? Maybe I *can* get him in, he's quite well known. Keating would arrange an interview for him, if I ask him to."

"Mm-hm."

"What's the matter, can't you talk? Would you rather call me back later?"

"No, I'm alone. I was thinking."

"Well, take your time!"

"It's a funny switch. He's got some reason for it," Forrest said. "Don't be surprised if it's a very personal one."

"How do you mean?" she asked, dismissing the obvious thing.

"You challenged him. I told you about that. You aren't afraid of him. He likes that."

"So what?"

"So go and find out," said Forrest. "I'll be around."

"Will I see you, while I'm there?"

"Very likely. Joanna will have me on any party list she draws up."

"Good. Maybe now we're getting some place."

"You're telling me?" His voice was grim.

"You don't sound pleased."

"It's too easy. Don't let him pull the rug out from under you."

"If I screamed could you hear me over at your house?" she asked, joking.

"No. Take down my home telephone number," he replied quite seriously, and gave it to her.

vii

SHE was not so closely in touch with Tad that he kept track of her week-ends, but it was with a faint guilt that she set out in Beaumont Marshall's car on Friday without having told anybody but Richie Forrest of her destination.

Marshall drove well and easily. His conversation was amusing and contained no pitfalls. When they arrived at his house in the late afternoon sunlight, Eve found it hard to reconcile this casual companion with the tricky, domineering man who had come to tea a few days before.

Joanna was waiting at the front door, and Eve kissed her anxious face with a gay greeting, and saw the quick, watchful glance Joanna sent towards her father. Obviously she had worried about the drive, and had been apprehensive about the state of mind in which their guest would arrive. She found only contentment on her father's face.

"Which room?" he was asking, Eve's bag in his hand.

"I thought — you said the lilac room," Joanna replied nervously. "At least, I put the flowers there, but — "

"*Boy!*" said Marshall, marching off with the bag up the staircase. "Miss Endicott's bag to the lilac room!"

Joanna looked after him with something like pride and a half-incredulous laugh.

"He used to clown like that quite a lot," she said in an undertone. "Margie Forrest used to say he ought to have been an actor. That always pleased him."

"What was she like?" Eve asked, standing still in the hall while her bag disappeared round a turn in the staircase.

"Margie?" Joanna looked at her consideringly. "She was the wisest, kindest woman in the world. With Margie around, things never got so bad — she usually knew how to manage him."

"How did her husband feel about that?" Eve asked.

"Oh, Richie didn't mind. There was never any question of who Margie *loved*. Sometimes, reading your books, I've thought you must be rather like her. *He's* noticed that too."

"But your father makes fun of my books!"

"He made fun of Margie too, for always believing the best of people, and things like that. It was a kind of contest between them — a game. He enjoyed it. She wasn't afraid of him. If only I was more like Margie I wouldn't exasperate him so. But I don't know how to play up to him the way she did, I get frightened and start to shake, and that infuriates him. Would you like to come up to your room now, or would you like some tea first?"

"I never refuse a cup of tea," Eve said thankfully.

"I thought so." Joanna was pleased. "In the drawing-room."

She led the way to the tea-table, where a silver kettle was already steaming over a spirit-lamp, and presided behind an imposing service with dignity and grace. They were laughing together when her father entered the room.

"*Tea?*" he said in playful surprise. "How about a drink?"

"Tea first, if you don't mind," Eve remarked with deliberate indifference, accepting her cup from Joanna's hand.

"Suppose I must wait, then." He took her refusal amiably, and approached the table.

"I made cress sandwiches," Joanna pointed out.

"Oh, well, in that case — " He carried the plate to Eve, and took a sandwich himself, sitting down beside her on the sofa to munch it. "What a domestic scene, Totsy, why don't we do this more often?"

"I'd be glad to, Father, but you're usually working at this time of day. I often have a cup of tea by myself," Joanna explained.

"Well, next time count me in. Maybe Miss Endicott will have a civilizing influence in other ways as well. Is that for me, you know I don't take sugar!"

Joanna dropped the spoon in the saucer with an undisciplined clatter, and the hunted look returned to her face.

"I'm s-sorry, it was for me, I thought you said — I didn't realize you wanted — " Fumbling a little, she made ready another cup without sugar and held it out to him. He took it with no further comment and settled back on the sofa beside Eve.

"W-was it a pleasant drive?" Joanna asked at random, snatching at a topic.

"Was it?" Marshall asked over his cup, of Eve.

"Delightful."

"I didn't behave abominably once, did I?" he insisted, holding her with his wide blue stare.

"I didn't expect you to."

"All is forgiven?" he pressed it, mock serious.

"Naturally."

"You see, Totsy?" he remarked triumphantly. "No harm done. We are so very anxious for you to think well of us, Miss Endicott," he added, with a certain underlining effect. "We have arranged a dinner party for this evening, in order to make a good impression. The McKenzies, the Hunters — and Joanna's would-be boyfriend from next door."

"Please, Father — " Joanna went white.

"You met Richie Forrest at Tad Benson's that Sunday, if you remember," Marshall went on smoothly to Eve, and she felt him watching her. "One of your strong, silent men. The women all fall for it. Would you say that I talked too much, Miss Endicott?"

"I haven't got a word in edgewise since I came!" she assured him lightly, and because this impudent, unpredictable man was unaware of any further communication between Forrest and herself since that Sunday she was foolishly uncomfortable beneath his searching eyes, and felt a tendency to disintegrate and stammer and fumble exactly as Joanna did. It might shake him up a bit to learn that she and Richie were already friends. She had an impulse to cast it in his teeth and suppressed it, for fear of awkward consequences to the harmless dinner party that evening. She wanted to see how long Marshall could keep this up. Already with the mention of Richie Forrest, the cold steel glinted in his voice again. She decided to play it safe, at least till Richie was in the house tonight.

"Suppose you give us in an unlimited number of words your first impressions of Joanna's middle-aged suitor," Marshall was saying in his dangerous purr. "Then after this evening you can furnish amendments and addenda."

"He's not — he's nothing of the sort!" cried Joanna

unwisely. "He only wants to be kind! It's no different than when Margie was alive!"

"I never said it was," said Marshall promptly, unable to resist that opening, and Joanna was miserably silent, sensing the innuendo, but not knowing how to deal with it. Eve suspected that even while he was still ignorant of the continued interest between herself and Forrest, some innate perversity moved Marshall to present the man next door to the least possible advantage. She gathered up her gloves and hand-bag in the silence.

"I think I'd like to go up to my room," she said briefly, and Marshall opened his eyes to their widest in profound innocence.

"What have I done now?" he begged humorously. "If you two are going to gang up on me every time I open my mouth — "

"Only when you put your foot in it," said Eve, and rose briskly.

"Are you on *his* side?" he demanded in grieved astonishment.

"I'm on Joanna's side." Eve put her arm around the girl, who had risen with her and was standing beside the tea-table, and she felt the slight body quivering with nerves. "And you may as well learn first as last that I hate it when you say things that are designed to upset her."

He sat looking up at them from the sofa, apparently

too struck with admiration and surprise to get to his feet as they turned and left the room together. It was an expression he had not worn since the last time Margie Forrest had set him back on his heels and left him there to cool.

viii

"I PROBABLY shouldn't have said that, will he sulk all evening now?" Eve asked as they reached the lilac room, and she drew Joanna inside and closed the door behind them.

Joanna sat down on the edge of the bed and fixed her eyes on the toes of her slippers.

"Miss Endicott, I don't want you to have a wrong impression about Richie Forrest," she said seriously. "I know I said in my letter that I was in love with him — and that's true in a way. At least, he's the most wonderful man I've ever known — gentle and kind and always tries to understand what you're saying. But I never had any idea of — I always knew he was in love with Margie and I hadn't any chance — " She caught her breath, and passed an unsteady hand across her face. "Miss Endicott, there's nobody else I can say this to. Would you mind?"

"Say anything you like, my dear." Eve took off her

hat and began to unpack. "I'll settle in a bit while we talk."

Joanna at once got to her feet distractedly.

"Perhaps I shouldn't — do you want to rest or — take a bath or — "

"No, no, you go right ahead. I'm just pottering." Eve waved her back and pretended to be busy at the bureau drawers.

"Well, I — you see, Margie was always wonderful to me, even though she must have known how I felt about Richie. She could afford to be, of course, she was perfectly sure that I didn't matter a hoot to him, beside her. There wasn't any doubt that they were happy together, and they had been married a long time. I knew that even if Margie were to — to die, he would never look twice at me. I was just the funny kid from next door who was always hanging around. I never *wished* for Margie to die, I always knew it wouldn't have been any good to me if she had, I — Miss Endicott, please listen."

"I'm listening. Every word. What you're really up against is a feeling that by loving Richie you unconsciously wished his wife out of the way, and then it happened."

"Y-yes. Almost as though — I'd killed her."

"That's natural enough, I think, in the circumstances," Eve conceded carefully. "At the same time, it's a morbid sort of idea and you mustn't allow it to stick, because of course there's nothing in it at all."

"You truly don't think there is?" Joanna's face was pathetic with hope.

"I truly don't. There's always a temptation to read significance into something that cancels out too neatly, like that. But it's wrong, Joanna, I've said it before and I say it again — you must make the most colossal allowance for coincidence in this life. Richie's wife died in a perfectly normal way."

"She was having a baby."

"Yes, but for her that was dangerous, and they knew it. She took a desperate gamble, and she lost. That's got nothing to do with you, and you must try to be sensible about it, my dear, it's very unhealthy to dwell on it." She came and put a friendly arm around Joanna's shoulders. "I don't mean to be too revoltingly rational, I know very well how these spooky notions can move in on you. But you really mustn't think like that, Joanna, it might affect your whole life, and Richie's."

"There's nothing in Richie's life for me now," Joanna said flatly. "While Margie was there I could see him without — without stretching it. Now, when he's living there alone, it's not the same."

"Yes, he told me about the time he took you in for a glass of sherry."

"He — told you?" Joanna stared at her.

"I didn't mention it down stairs just now, but Richie and I have seen each other in town since that Sunday at Tad's — lunch, you know, just for laughs. We liked each other. Now, don't look like that, I don't have to be in love with a man to have lunch with him!"

"Miss Endicott — please don't let Father know."

"Well, I didn't. But why not?"

"Because I'm pretty sure he's fallen in love with you."

"*My dear Joanna — !*"

"I know it must sound crazy to you, and I probably shouldn't have brought it up, but I couldn't help noticing, and you didn't seem to. It's the way you talk to him — the way you don't care what he thinks — that off-hand way you have with him — that was Margie's way too. That's what he likes."

"But surely other women besides Margie and me have brushed him off!"

"He scares people. He *tries* to," Joanna said miserably.

"Well, I admit I don't scare very easy, especially in broad daylight — "

"Please, Miss Endicott, don't laugh it off, it's serious."

Eve sat down on the bed beside her.

"Perhaps in the circumstances you'd better call me Eve. Why can't I laugh if I want to?"

"You must never laugh *at* him. Margie said so. She warned me."

"Joanna, we're getting pretty well down to bedrock here. May I ask a simple question? Was he in love with Margie?"

"But that was it, don't you see?" Joanna said simply. "And Richie had her, and she wanted it that way. Father hadn't a hope, any more than I had. He knew that, he was used to it, he wasn't even trying to change it. But he needed her in his life — like a balance-wheel. When she died like that, he blamed Richie. He hates Richie, because Margie is dead."

Eve rose from the edge of the bed, and pushed back her hair with a wide, reckless gesture.

"Phewie!" she said expressively. "I'm glad I'm not writing this one!"

"But you are," said the soft, insistent voice from the bed, and Eve spun round.

"How's that again?"

"Now that you've come, anything can happen," Joanna said. "It's all up to you now."

"Here, here, just a minute," Eve began hastily. "I've only come for a week-end, I — " She stopped. A bit late to talk like that, wasn't it. She was the girl who was going to re-write the rest of Joanna's life. By a few simple, tactful words, and a discreet amount of interference, all without raising anybody's voice, she was going to save Joanna. It didn't sound so easy now when Joanna said it.

"What I started to say was," Joanna pursued in her gentle, inexorable way, "don't make him jealous—with Richie, I mean. Because this time it's not the same. Margie was married to Richie before they ever came here."

"But why should you assume—" Eve struggled for coherence. "Joanna, I live a very dull life. I only write novels, people our age don't go round dropping into love at first sight in any kind of set-up!"

"The way you spoke to him down stairs just now—the way he looked at you—it was like an echo," Joanna said obstinately.

"Echo? You mean I'm standing in for Margie here?" Eve was conscious of a slight prickle along her spine.

"Well, I don't know if Richie has noticed it. But we have."

"Noticed *what?*"

"How very much like her you are. You don't *look* like her, it's not that, it's just something about the way you are. That's a compliment," Joanna added anxiously, as Eve stood perfectly still, gazing at her in a stunned silence. "Everybody adored Margie."

With a definite physical effort to gather herself together Eve swung away to the mirror. A rather dazed face looked back at her, but it was still her own face, the same one she had seen in her own mirror that morning. *I don't know if Richie has noticed it*, Joanna had said. Perhaps, Eve thought, she was sounding like an echo to Richie too. . . .

She felt suddenly as though her own identity were oozing away. How could one *not* remind these people of Margie? Where was the line between her own inviolate self and Margie's — reflection? Not to be afraid of Beau Marshall was Margie. To be sane and loving with Joanna was Margie. To feel a sort of quickening when Richie was near — that was Margie too. I'd better get out of here, Eve thought, looking into the mirror. I'd better —

She was conscious that Joanna had moved and was standing beside her.

"Please don't ever let Father know that I gave him away," she whispered. "He'll tell you himself pretty soon, I expect. But I thought I ought to say — while you're here don't take much notice of Richie."

"No, nor of your father either, I should think," said Eve. "What other men will there be to concentrate on?"

"It might sound as though I was speaking on my own account, about Richie," Joanna went on breathlessly. "But it's not that. I had to separate you at the table tonight — but don't think it's because I wanted Richie to myself. I just knew it would be better that way."

Eve laid both hands on Joanna's shoulders, looking into the sweet, trusting, troubled face.

"Dear Joanna, so far as I'm concerned, both these guys are all yours! Maybe I shouldn't have come here at all.

I thought I could help you if I did. I wanted to get you out of this *cocoon* into a life of your own, with or without Richie Forrest. Instead, I am beginning to feel as though it's being spun around me too. But I'm not Margie Forrest, remember that. I haven't any intention of being like her. I'm Eve, I write books, I don't belong here. See?"

Joanna put her arms around Eve, and Eve felt the soft cool hair against her face, and the slim weightless body hugging hers.

"But it's so much nicer since you came," Joanna whispered, and was gone from the room with a soundless closing of the door behind her.

Eve had a hot bath and put on a fresh face and dressed for dinner, still in a haze. Her own words still resounded in the quiet room — *I'm not Margie Forrest — I haven't any intention of being like her.* Go away, Margie Forrest. But Margie was gone — they said. That was the trouble.

As the shadows gathered in the corners of the lilac room and Eve snapped on the lights over the dressing-table, it took some will power to dismiss the hovering idea that Margie had not gone very far — that she was still so alive and important in the minds of these people who had been so profoundly influenced by her, that something more than her memory still lingered here with them, watching, listening, waiting — for an understudy? A little trickle of nerves ran down Eve's spine again. No, you don't, Margie Forrest. I'm getting out of here.

She looked forward shamelessly to Richie's arrival for dinner, though his presence promised to be another problem in itself. There must be some way to find out if his own quick interest in Eve Endicott was also because of Margie, and if it was, Eve wanted no part in it from now on. I will not be pushed around by anybody's ghost, she told herself crazily, pinching on her earrings before the mirror. I'm not Margie, and I'm not going to stooge for her. I'm Eve Endicott or else.

But she dawdled till she heard cars in the driveway and voices in the lower hall, and then descended to the drawing-room to find the dinner-party assembled. The men looked fresh and shaved and prosperous in their dinner jackets, and the wives wore gay, low-cut dresses, and Joanna was a fair-haired schoolgirl in white.

Cocktails went round, and then Eve was seated at the candle-lit table on Marshall's right, with the rather ponderous Mr. McKenzie on her other side — and was cross with herself for remembering at once that damaging remark of Marshall's at Tad's about McKenzie's secretary. There was no reason for it to be true, his wife was an attractive woman. But it had stuck, as such things have a way of doing.

Eve had been presented to Marshall's other guests rather like a visiting queen, and as the meal progressed she was conscious of his continuing effort to spotlight her, and to call attention to his devoted personal interest in his new acquaintance. He was, as Joanna's second letter had specified, very charming, very good-looking, very amusing, and he did not drink too much.

Responding almost automatically to his practiced lead, Eve found the memory of that awful afternoon in New York receding like the memory of a nightmare. Mindful of Richie's account of other dinner-parties where Joanna had been deliberately reduced to tears, Eve tried to watch and listen for signs of similar disaster tonight, and there weren't any. Joanna, with Richie on her right, wore a touching glow of happiness, and forgot to glance at her father for permission to speak. The table talk flowed smoothly, and the excellent food came and went without a hitch. It was a delightful and well-ordered meal, and Beaumont Marshall was an exceptional host.

Just once during the meal Eve dared to catch Richie Forrest's eye, and allowed a momentary expression of comic bewilderment to flit across her face. In the same split second, his left eyelid flickered in the briefest possible wink. I can't *wait,* Eve heard herself telling herself, to get him on the phone in town on Monday. She couldn't, of course, penetrate the good manners of the Hunters and the McKenzies to the frantic speculation overtaking each one of them as to the reason for

Marshall's good humor, and their growing conviction that she alone was in some way responsible.

To everyone's surprise, the fair weather lasted out the entire evening, which broke up a little earlier than usual because Mrs. Hunter and Mrs. McKenzie couldn't wait to get their husbands alone for an exchange of views. Richie Forrest took a graceful leave with the rest, and the other three were left in a friendly afterglow.

They drifted towards the sofas which stood end on to the fireplace, and Joanna began to collect ashtrays and empty glasses with housewifely care. Eve suppressed the first unself-conscious impulse to help her and sat down instead, which brought her under Marshall's steady, smiling regard as he stood on the hearthrug.

"Don't domesticate, Totsy, come and sit down," he commanded pleasantly over his shoulder, without taking his eyes off Eve. "Let's all have a little nightcap together."

"Nothing for me, thanks," said Eve, hoping to escape to her room as soon as possible.

"Just a teeny one," he coaxed, going to the tray where the liquor and glasses were. "Rye for you, wasn't it? Scotch for little me. And a drop of crème de menthe for Totsy. *If* she can find us some clean glasses?"

"Oh — just a second — I'll get some — " Joanna flew off, lightfooted and happy, towards the kitchen.

Marshall waited beside the tray, leaning on the back of

a chair, watching Eve on the sofa across the room.

"I like the way you look in my house," he said, very low. "I like your being here, when all the others have gone. Did you enjoy yourself tonight?'"

"Very much. Such nice people," she said impersonally.

"Surprised?" he purred, with his uncomfortable faculty of pressing a point.

"Not at all."

"Liar."

"I never doubted that you could behave, if you wanted to," she told him severely. "That only makes it worse when you don't."

"Why do I want to when you are here? I'm afraid you bring out the best in me, Miss Endicott."

"That's good," she said carelessly.

"Eve. There's a lot in a name, sometimes." He left a long silence which she would not break. "May I say Eve from now on?"

"If you like."

"Eve," he murmured, motionless, watching her. "The first and only woman in the world. The original mystery."

"Oh, come, now, Mr. Marshall, that's not — "

"I thought we had agreed on first names."

"But yours is so — theatrical," she complained with a humorous, despairing gesture.

"I know. My mother's maiden name, I come by it

honestly, but she never should have wished it on me. You could call me something else — if you can think of anything you prefer."

"I was never much good at nicknames."

"You're an excellent duellist, aren't you, Eve? So few women are. They lose their heads, and giggle or get angry. I've only known one other like you, and I loved her very much. Don't misunderstand me. She was not my wife." Again he paused, and she made no comment. "I promised myself that if ever I met her equal I would have her, come hell or high water. It was an easy vow to make, because it seemed so improbable at the time." He had not moved from his easy position behind the chair, his elbows on its back, and his voice was pitched so that it barely reached her on the sofa. She found herself listening tensely, unwillingly, for each word. "It begins to look as though I would have to make good on it, after all," he said, and then Joanna came back through the dim, deserted dining-room with glasses tinkling on a tray. "Oh, there you are, Joanna," he said casually, and left the chair. "I hoped you had gone to bed."

"I — you said you wanted glasses — I had to wash them — I brought more ice — "

"That was very clever of you." Smiling, he took the tray from her hands. "Rye — Scotch — crème de menthe — coming up!"

ix

JOANNA lay awake in the dark, recalling her dinner-party in each magic detail. It was, so far, the social triumph of her precarious life. Not once had her father's glance flickered over her in derisive unspoken comment, not once had he challenged her modest efforts at conversation. Richie had sat beside her, smiling and content, not bored, not uneasy, and always ready to understand what she was trying to say — so kind, so good, so willing to be her friend. It was all she wanted — just to see him sometimes like that. Well — all she ever expected to *have*. She could do with that. She had never hoped for more.

She lay very quiet, hearing her own heartbeats like thunder, daring herself to contemplate the more — like that day he had taken her into his car and driven round till she stopped crying and acting like a baby — only he hadn't said she was acting like a baby, he had pretended it was perfectly normal for one to be wandering about the streets with tears running down one's face. And then he had invited her into his house for a glass of sherry, just as though she was somebody, and when he brought it to her — the bell-shaped glass small and fragile in his big brown hand — he had looked down at her and said, "How nice to see you here again. I've missed you — along with a lot of other pleasant things." Not a very impressive compliment, perhaps, but it was the best she had ever had.

She had found it quite natural and easy to sit facing him in the familiar quiet living-room with her glass of sherry, while he drank whiskey and water — not strange at all, to talk to him all on her own, without Margie there to give her confidence. She had even made him laugh, with a little story about two old ladies at the bus stop. He looked tired, and very lonely. She wondered how he bore it to go on living there, when everything he saw and touched must remind him of all he had lost. And yet what else could people do when someone they loved had died? Shut up a whole house, sell it, lose contact forever with a happiness which had once been real, just because it was over?

Joanna knew that everyone had been waiting to see what he would do about the house where Margie had lived. At first there was talk that he would sell it and go into bachelor quarters somewhere. When he didn't, they began to speculate about his marrying again. But since that afternoon when he had given her the sherry just as though nothing had changed, Joanna thought that he was doing the bravest and hardest thing of all — he was sitting it out with his grief, in the belief that finally his memories would become bearable and even comforting — because Margie had made a home, and even without her that was still there.

When Joanna came to her father's eruption into that afternoon, and the humiliating scene he had made, implying that she had planned to meet Richie and that they had tried to do something underhand and scandalous with Richie's car standing right there in broad daylight to advertise his return home, she switched her mind hastily back to the dinner-party which had gone so smoothly tonight, as though it was customary for eight people to gather round that table, Richie among them. All thanks to Eve Endicott. Joanna perceived that Eve's influence was going to be an enormous factor in their lives from now on. Richie had noticed it too, during dinner.

"What's going on around here?" he had asked in an undertone as the salad came in, with a glance at her father's relaxed, smiling face. "We're all full of sweetness and light."

"Oh, Richie, it's like a miracle!"

"Will it last, do you think?"

"Oh, I hope so. I hope she doesn't turn him down!"

Richie looked at her with visible surprise.

"It's not got as far as that, has it?" he asked.

"It will, I know it will. He's in love with her, Richie, he must be! He's — all lit up inside. Wouldn't it be wonderful if we could keep her here — "

"How about her?" Richie said. "Isn't it rather a tall order, and isn't it rather sudden?"

"Yes, I know. But he can be awfully good company when he wants to. Oh, Richie, I've prayed for something like this to happen!"

"I know you have," he said compassionately. "But it's a bit late now, isn't it?"

"I've still got my life to live, Richie."

"Yes, it would certainly make things easier for you," he conceded. "But don't count on it, Joanna. Miss Endicott has a life of her own, don't forget — she's not one to be swept off her feet. Better men have doubtless tried before now."

Looking back in the small hours, Joanna began to have qualms. Richie and Miss Endicott had lunched together. Suppose Richie was falling in love with her. There was no question in Joanna's mind that Richie could win any woman he wanted. Suppose Eve chose Richie instead. It didn't bear thinking about — but not, Joanna at once assured herself, because she had any chance with Richie herself.

She pulled the pillow over her head and longed for sleep. Tomorrow was full of complications. Richie had suggested casually, before them all, that the Marshalls bring Miss Endicott to tea at his house tomorrow afternoon. His married brother was driving down from Hartford and his brother's wife Stella was a brilliant pianist — he could promise them some music, and his English cook was famous for her scones. They had accepted the invitation, and Joanna thought she was looking forward to it. But not if her father was going to collide with Richie over Miss Endicott. Not if the miracle didn't hold . . .

In the house next door, Richie Forrest was trying without success to read himself to sleep, although he had laid aside one of Eve's volumes and replaced it with something duller. The evening had given him too much to think about. Joanna had blossomed before his eyes into a radiant young woman, with a quaint and somehow heartrending dignity. He had seen, as though for the first time, the high carriage of her head on its slim neck, the childish swing of her brushed hair against her cheeks, her upward, lingering look which said so plainly that in her meager world he came first. It was a new and disturbing sensation, to see Joanna as a woman. She was already dear to him. But now Eve Endicott had said, out of the blue, *You could marry her*. And tonight it came home to him, hard, that he could.

Inevitably, he thought of Margie. And it seemed to him, lying with the forgotten book in his hands, looking through it into the unfinished story of Joanna's life, that Margie gave her free consent to this escape for the girl they had both longed to rescue. Eve had said it, but Margie could have spoken. His mind dwelt affectionately on Eve. He knew, because he was not a fool, that the spark had been struck between them, and that he might even now sail in and take her away from Tad Benson. She was a remarkably footloose and self-sufficient young woman, financially secure, accustomed to her widowhood. She had no need for marriage except love. Joanna knew very little about love, but marriage was her only hope. He felt again the old, familiar tug of Joanna's helplessness and trust.

Richie recognized the crossroads with his customary honesty. As of now he was a man with a choice. To try and win Eve Endicott would be an exciting adventure which might end in failure. In any case, it would mean a lot of innovation and adjustment for both of them. She had never even been inside his home. It was unlikely that she would be willing to live there, as a second wife; she would want her own setting, with everything new. There was no way to be sure about that, of course, till it was too late to retreat. And would he be willing to uproot, start again, create a new background, begin new traditions, with a stranger? Joanna, already won, belonged in the house, belonged in all the old traditions, was unself-conscious and predictable about Margie and his memories.

Tomorrow they would both be here in his house at tea-time, and so would Beau Marshall — and it was obvious that Marshall considered himself in the running too. The idea brought to Richie a swift recurrence of the same small chill which had overtaken him twice before — when Eve on the telephone had told him of this week-end invitation, and again at dinner tonight when Joanna had expressed the childish hope that Eve would not turn Beau down.

It was thoughtless of Joanna to be willing that Eve should be caught in the emotional quicksands of the Marshall household, and Richie assured himself that Eve was much too clever to be taken in by Beau's good moods. But — *he can be awfully good company when he wants to*, Joanna had said. Even Margie, who saw through everybody as though they were made of plate glass, had more than once said the same thing. Even Margie had wished, in the goodness of her heart, that some wise, loving woman would undertake Beau's salvation in time.

But not Eve, Richie thought, entertaining again that small chill. You couldn't wish it on Eve. Besides, Beau was getting much worse lately. Except tonight. In all fairness, tonight was rather a miracle, as Joanna had said. Might it not begin to look easy to Eve, after tonight, so that she set about rescuing Marshalls right and left? Because then somebody would have to rescue Eve.

Once he had lightly alleged to Margie that if she had not already been spoken for, she would herself have been fool enough to take on the Marshalls as a lifework out of sheer charity and natural born meddlesomeness. And Margie had replied, with her face against his, that he never had to speak very loud, had he — and now the long, cramping pain which was Margie's endless absence wrenched through him again. I don't know what to do, he acknowledged, when it had run its course. I can't save them both from him. Eve is old enough to know better. But she is like Margie, she has both compassion and spirit, she'll tackle anything. . . .

The unuttered words paused in his mind, while he contemplated them with astonishment. Like Margie. . . . He had not thought of it before. There was no outward resemblance. But the fire and the tenderness — they were the same. If Beau had noticed that too it might be the reason for Eve's immediate effect on him — some demented idea that he might still possess in Eve the essence of what he had desired in Margie. To Richie, lying sleepless in his empty house, it was an unhappy idea. One could hardly suggest such a thing to Eve, not without sounding psychic and ridiculous. But if he couldn't cut Beau Marshall out with Eve he would eat his hat. And then what became of Joanna?

In any case, the situation between himself and Eve must be faced at once, and some decision arrived at, at least on his own part, with no hanging about on one foot. He must go either forward or back with Eve, she was that kind of woman. Not fair to either of them not to know his own mind. Tomorrow. Tomorrow he would decide. He tried to think, as he turned out the light, that his choice was still to be made. . . .

In the lilac room across the hall from Joanna's, Eve reached out irritably and snapped her light back on, and picked up the book she had laid on the bedside table half an hour before. Sleep was apparently impossible, she might as well give it up. The type blurred before her dazzled eyes, and she closed them impatiently to accustom them to the light. It was a mistake to start reading again after lying awake in the dark. Likewise it was a mistake to lie awake in the dark. She was ready to admit to herself now that perhaps her presence in Beau Marshall's house was a mistake from beginning to end.

Certainly it had turned the hard-won orderliness of her private life into something like civil war. Richie Forrest had come to dinner, and it mattered to her much too much that he had hardly taken his eyes off Joanna all evening. It was implicit, of course, that he should show no interest in Eve while Marshall was looking, but hadn't he overdone it a bit? No, she shouted inwardly at herself, of course he hadn't, he was absorbed in Joanna just as he should have been!

The idea was to give Joanna a chance to show the enchanting creature she was meant to be, especially to the man who was meant to rescue her. What kind of fairy godmother was it, who begrudged the very magic she had set herself to bring about? Tonight's dinner party had been a greater success than Eve had dared to expect. In Richie Forrest's eyes Joanna had at last ceased to be the kid next door and had shone as a competent hostess and a delightful young woman. Joanna was now competition for anyone else Richie might contemplate. Joanna was half way to the happy ending, as she would not have been if Eve Endicott had minded her own business as she was advised to do.

Without the new script thrown into the scales nothing would have happened. With it she had hooked Beau Marshall. Tomorrow morning he would show her his illustration layout, and she would have to be non-committal and discreet, no matter how good it was — but with praise, whether she liked it or not. Continued negotiations on the illustrating job kept the door open for Joanna's escape into the world beyond her father's tyranny.

Eve began to dread the interview in the studio tomorrow in a new and unexpected way. He had not interfered tonight with Joanna's modest triumph, and if she had never seen him in any other circumstances Eve would have considered him one of the most charming men she had ever met. That word. The word Joanna had used, deliberately damning, in her letter. Well, it was the right word tonight, Eve had seldom seen it better embodied. The man had wit and intelligence and masculine magnetism. It was a pity he had elected to waste it all on a pose of embittered cynicism. She weighed that word too, asking herself which was the pose — the man who came to tea, or the man who had entertained them all at dinner tonight? And then she came to those few minutes at the end of the evening, while Joanna was in the kitchen. Did he think she was born yesterday? She couldn't let him get away with an obvious line like that, and she had parried him briskly at the time, even taken by surprise as she had been.

But now she contemplated the incident with a growing curiosity, wondering if he would begin there tomorrow morning, or if it had been just the mellowing effect of the late hour and the emptied, intimate room. First names, anyhow. He had established a beachhead there. She reminded herself mercilessly that no woman, especially one past her first youth, can remain quite impervious to genuine admiration openly expressed. It was always comforting, on the far side of thirty, Eve insisted to herself, only to learn once more that one is still attractive. How readily one responds, she thought ruefully, with what pitiful willingness, to new evidence of anything that could be love. Even from Beau Marshall?

But she had no impulse to ridicule the idea now. Something had happened to Beau Marshall tonight. Perhaps it was that he had finally realized the futility — and the awful loneliness — of trying to live with every man's hand against him and his against every man. Suppose — just suppose, someone had the courage and the know-how to love Beau Marshall, as Margie, without Richie, might have done. Suppose, even now, someone tried to write a happy ending for Beau Marshall. . . .

There it is again, Eve thought, just as she slid into sleep, with the light still on. As though I was not *myself* any more — as though it was Margie who holds the pen now, and is writing this thing instead of me. I must get out of here, Eve thought — I must get away from Margie. . . .

At the end of the hall, the master's bedroom where Joanna's father slept was quiet and dark.

X

JOANNA was already behind the coffee urn when Eve arrived in the dining-room the next morning, and her host rose gallantly from his own place to draw back her chair. His wide gaze was merry and knowing, as though they shared some secret understanding from the night before.

"No need to ask if either of you slept well," he said as she sat down. "A bonnier brace of gals I never did see. I'm a *very* lucky man, and I only hope it lasts!"

"Touch wood!" said Joanna, laughing.

"And watch yourself," said Eve, returning his look coolly.

"I'm trying," he replied, quite serious.

"You're doing all right," she acknowledged. "So far."

Breakfast passed uneventfully, except that the general good will seemed to go to Joanna's head, so that she chattered like a schoolgirl. Eve encouraged her, and her father watched them both with an air of indulgence amounting to approval.

When they rose from the table he led the way at once to the studio, and Joanna stayed behind in conference with the cook.

Eve looked round the big, cluttered room with interest. A few framed oils which looked as though they had been done on European holidays, some black and white studies pinned to the walls, an easel, a model's throne, a large work-table in front of one window, stacks of black portfolios against the walls with the rough edges of sketches showing.

"What a nice workshop," she said easily. "Not a bit arty."

"I have my failings," he admitted, "but throwing my weight around about my job is not one of them. I'm just a nice, reliable hard-working hack when it comes to that."

She went to the table where the layout was, in color, and he stood watching her while she took it in. To her great relief it was more than good, it was bold, original, expertly done, and very striking. The upturned, expectant face of the woman was her own, made a little younger to fit the story, and with chestnut hair cut like hers.

"Well, you *have* got a nerve!" she said first of all, trying to keep it light.

"Are you cross?" he murmured.

"On the contrary, it's very flattering. How could you get such a likeness on such short acquaintance?"

"I could make a lot of high-falutin answers to that." He came around the table to stand behind her, looking over her shoulder. "The simple truth is, I couldn't get you out of my mind. Eve — " His arm came round her, and when she moved to elude it he caught and held her, her face pressed against his shoulder, and she felt the hard, heavy pump of his heart and a trembling through his body. "Eve, please — I want you — "

For a moment she stood quite still in his embrace, knowing better than to try to break it, rejecting the first things which occurred to her to say. The whole day, perhaps a great deal more than just today, hung on her ability to handle wisely this crisis which had come sooner than she expected. Perhaps that was the line to take — unless to pretend surprise after last evening . . .

"Aren't you — rushing it a bit?" she asked as calmly as she could, and felt his hold slacken reluctantly so that she moved back away from him till the edge of the table stopped her.

"I suppose I am," he said quite reasonably. "The last few days haven't seemed as long to you as they did to me, waiting for this. Eve — " He caught at her hands, and she gave a nervous, involuntary glance at the door.

"Please be careful — "

"Joanna doesn't come in here unless she's sent for. "Eve — "

"Now, stop it, Beau, we're both grown up, sensible people." She slid away from him, along the table, and he let her go, looking obedient and chidden. "I like your picture — I like it very much. I'll speak to Keating about it. He has the script now."

"You know I don't give a damn about the picture, don't you. No, that's not correct. I do give a damn because I'd like to have the private personal satisafaction of working with you. But it's not the money or the field of illustrating any more — it's you." He stood patiently at the end of the sofa. "Please come and sit down, Eve. You don't have to keep the whole room between us." He waited till she took the extreme farthest end, and then sat down himself, casually, in the middle, but not touching her. "I appreciate your self-restraint," he said with faint irony. "You didn't laugh in my face, anyway."

"That wouldn't have been very polite, would it? On such a lovely morning, too."

"Polite, she says! If I hadn't read your books I'd think it was all an act. But it isn't, is it." He leaned forward to look into her face. "I used to think you were just whistling past the graveyard. But you're not kidding, are you. To you, the world looks like that, all the time. You couldn't keep it up like this if it wasn't real. Eve — ?"

"How could I be any different than I *am*?" She

threw out both hands in exasperation. "What do you expect? What on earth kind of women have you known?"

"The usual kind. Except one. And now you."

"You ought to get around more. There are dozens like me."

"That's the first stupid remark I've ever heard you make."

"Well, give me time. I've got lots more."

He laughed quietly, sitting still in the middle of the sofa beside her.

"How good it is to hear someone talk like that again!" he said unguardedly, and she knew she must by accident have sounded like Margie. But surely she had only sounded like herself. A little more and she would accuse him outright of confusing her with Margie. He leaned forward and took one of her hands, holding it tightly in both his, looking down at their intertwined fingers. "Eve — stick around, won't you? Don't let me go mad."

"Oh, my dear — !" Her free hand flew out to join the others, and he bent to lay his lips against it in mute appeal. "You mustn't talk like that," she said gently, leading with her heart again, when she knew she should have kept him at arm's length. "You've built up this thing in your mind — but you don't know anything about me, really — you've got a false sense of familiarity by reading the stuff I write, but that doesn't tell you anything much about *me*, it's only the way I make my living — "

"Shut up," he said tensely, and raised his head so that she saw his strange, brilliant eyes blurred with tears. "Who cares what you write, or what I draw? Oh, sure, your books got at me first, before I ever set eyes on you. I wanted to laugh at them, I tried to think they were tripe designed for simple minds like Joanna's — but it wasn't as easy as it should have been. When I saw you I knew why. It's because you haven't any act at all — you're *real*."

"What's so difficult about that?" she inquired, deliberately matter-of-fact. "Joanna's real. *You're* real — aren't you?"

"No, of course I'm not. Perhaps I could have been. Perhaps I could be still — if it mattered enough."

"Why do you do it, Beau? Why do you let the demon take over, when you can be the way you were last evening?"

"That's not the point," he said doggedly. "The point is, would it matter to you?"

"Well, I — I don't — "

"Because if it doesn't, the hell with it," he said, and dropped her hands and rose restlessly. "You don't know what a strain last evening was for me," he added, and eyed her from the middle of the room with a kind of triumph. "I was bound I'd do it — just to show you I could. And I succeeded, didn't I! I didn't behave abominably once, did I! Were you impressed?"

"I was *very* impressed!" she agreed, humoring him. "But why must it be such an effort? It didn't look hard."

He gave a disarming boyish snicker.

"Almost killed me," he said, wandering around the middle of the room with his hands in his pockets, while she watched him with an unwilling fascination. "I wasn't sure I still had it in me. Don't you see how it is?" He faced her and cast wide his arms in an embracing, theatrical gesture. "For you I can do anything! Does that mean anything at all to you? Because if it doesn't, I shan't bother. It's much easier not."

"But *why* is it, Beau? Why should it be easier to make everybody uncomfortable than to have things go well?"

"You answer my question first," he insisted humorously.

"Well, I — when you're like this, anything is possible, but — "

"Say it again!" With a quick, unexpected movement he was beside her on the sofa, both her hands caught in his. "Eve, let me hear that again!"

"Now, wait a minute, please, I only — "

"You said it!" he cried gaily. "You said anything was possible! That's all I wanted to know!"

"Now Beau, hold it, I only — "

He kissed her. The swift, urgent contact tingled

through her before she could push him away, and as he let her go he said lightly, "Just for luck. Don't slay me," and she laughed a little, moved in spite of herself by this new defenceless mood of his, unwilling to be too hard on him, but determined things should go no farther. "What's funny?" he demanded, and at once his eyes were wary and his hands loosened.

"Me," she said hastily. "Just me, getting kissed like a teen-ager. I thought I had more sense." She rose, and he made no effort to stop her. "Joanna will be wondering — "

"It's no affair of Joanna's what goes on in here," he said flatly. "This room is out of bounds for Joanna. She learned that long ago." His tone made her pause.

"How?" she asked, trying to sound casual. "How did she learn?"

"By trial and error, like a white mouse." It was plain he had no intention of enlightening her. The wild defiant look was on him again. His eyes were bright and shallow, his mouth curved in his cold, closed smile.

"Why are you like that about Joanna?" Eve said, standing still. "Why does it amuse you to terrorize her?"

"She asks for it. I like a little spirit in a woman."

"That's no reason, Beau," she said ruefully.

"Well, then, she's the image of her mother. That's as far as it goes — I hope. If I see any signs of the rest of it, I'll put her in a nunnery."

"Why don't you let all that old bitterness go?" Eve said earnestly, and laid one hand on his sleeve. "Try to forget it. It happened, it's over, she's gone. She doesn't matter any more. The same thing has happened to a lot of other people."

"I've heard that before. In almost the same words." He was motionless under her hand.

"I'm sure you have. It's a very obvious thing to say. But very true."

"From only one other person, Eve. The only other person I ever cared a damn about."

"Well, then, it ought to make all the more sense to you now."

"You don't ask me who that was."

"Does it matter?"

"I think it does. It was Richie Forrest's wife. I want you to know about that, Eve. I was in love with Richie Forrest's wife. But don't get me wrong. Margie was a saint. There was nothing — " He turned away, trying to steady his voice. " — Nothing — "

"It was bad luck, Beau — that she was somebody else's wife. She must have been a very — exceptional person. But she wouldn't want you to go to pieces like this."

"For fifteen years I had to see them together — *happy* together — not wanting anything but to *be* together. I tried to play fair at first, but then I would have taken her away from him if I could. Joanna felt the same pull, she deserted to them every chance she got — Margie said I kept Joanna too close, *she was all I had!* At night I used to watch their lights — the ones down stairs would go out — the ones upstairs would come on — and go out — "

"Beau — don't — it's finished now — " She stood behind him, her hands on his sleeves.

"That's what I mean," he said, not moving under her hands. "That's what I mean about you. You don't hesitate to give me hell when I deserve it. But you know when the chips are down — and then you don't laugh — you don't tell me to buck up and be gay — you don't even offer me anything instead — anything but compassion. There's very little of that around these days, did you know? Margie had it — that's why she put up with me. And it's in your books — in your voice — in your hands — " He laid his over them, holding them on his sleeves.

The little warning prickle ran down Eve's spine again. She tried too late to draw away, tried to step back out of Margie's tracks once more, and he shook his head, and turning, caught her by the shoulders, looking down.

"She promised me there was someone like you," he whispered. "If I was a good boy and always ate my spinach. You're late, Eve. It's been years. What kept you?" His arms closed in.

"I — you've no right — " She began to back away

from him. "It makes me feel like a parcel left under the Christmas tree! *To Beau—from Margie, with love.* I don't like it—I d-don't—you can't—" She was beginning to stammer and flutter. He reached for her unwisely and she broke away and ran for the door. "*No*—it's too soon—I can't—" The door swung open under her hand, and she glanced back. He was standing where she had left him, in the middle of the room, looking after her.

On her way to the stairs she ran into Joanna, who took instant alarm at the sight of her face.

"What is it? Didn't you like the picture? Is he furious?"

"No, he's not furious at all. I—liked the picture very much and—I told him so." Eve caught her breath and strove for composure.

"Oh, you *didn't* turn him down!" wailed Joanna. "Oh, Eve, don't ever leave us, it's so different with you here!"

"Joanna, I came here for the week-end." Eve spoke very calmly by main force. "I have no intention of making a lifework of the Marshall family." She began to ascend the stairs. Her knees felt queer, and her heart was pounding.

"Please don't be angry." Joanna came up swiftly behind her, and laid an arm around her waist. "If he'd asked my advice I'd have told him not to ask you so soon. I guess he forgot how it might seem to you, because to us it seems so *inevitable*—Eve, I hope you didn't upset him—"

"*I* am the one who is upset," Eve told her sharply. "That will be a change for him, won't it!"

And she went into her room and closed the door.

xi

JOANNA stood there a minute in the passage outside Eve's door. Then she leaned over the bannister and looked down at the closed door of her father's studio. While she hung there he opened it and looked out into the hall. She came down a few steps, uncertainly, and he noticed her.

"Well?" he asked abruptly. "Did you see her? What did she say?"

"She's gone and shut herself into her room. She was upset."

"I gathered that." But his smile was rueful and not unfriendly. "Want to help?"

"Yes, of course." She came down another step.

"You stay right here. Just in case she packs her bag and sends for a taxi. And if she does try to leave the house hang on to her and yell till I come." He turned back towards the studio and Joanna sat down on the step.

"Father — do you mind my saying — " She was peering at him through the railings like a child. " — I couldn't help noticing — you're in love with her, aren't you."

"Sh, not so loud! She hasn't an idea!" It was his old, bantering manner, and she sensed a mood where it was safe to go on.

"Didn't you ask her to marry you just now?"

He stood stock still, staring up at her.

"Well, now that you mention it — no," he said.

"But I th-thought — "

"Yes — you thought." He was still riveted. "Yes — that figures. Out of the mouths of babes. Thank you, Totsy, for reminding me." He passed her on the stairs, two at a time, and came to a stop in front of the closed door. "Eve," he said, and tapped on the panel. "Eve, I've come to apologize — " Laughter broke through the words, in his most charming way. But there was no reply, no sound, from within. "I forgot something, Eve. Couldn't we get on speaking terms before lunch?"

"Go away. I'm thinking."

"I could help."

"Later."

He came back to the stairs, and Joanna's anxious face looking up at him.

"Shall I try?" she whispered.

"Let's wait." He sat down beside her on the step, and took out a cigarette.

So the Marshall family, seated companionably on the stairs, drawn together by a common need, settled down to sweat it out till Eve's door opened.

Joanna was speechless, wondering what had happened between them in the studio, afraid to ask, or risk damaging the bond of friendly conspiracy which Eve's displeasure had created. He had not ordered her away, he had not said it was none of her business. He was here, within reach of her hand, lively and amused and in some secret way enjoying himself, and willing that she should share his mood. The usual humiliating gratitude flooded through her. She could never afford not to welcome his fair weather, or be slow to respond to his least opening, because to cherish a grudge or hold out for an apology from him meant forfeiting the only company she had, which was his. So she sat silent beside him while he smoked, glad of his proximity, waiting for him to indicate the next move.

He finished his cigarette, stubbed it out against the bottom of his shoe, laid the butt on the end of the step between the railings, and turned a quizzical glance on his daughter.

"I goofed," he said, and she laughed readily at his unexpected use of slang she had no idea he knew. "An old-timer like me," he added, shaking his head.

"It seems so natural to have her here, I expect you went

too fast," Joanna ventured. "Because of her books, and because of Margie, it's only natural we should feel that we know her much better than we really do. You see," she explained earnestly, forgetting to stammer or choose her words in the generous effort to restore face to him, "we have the advantage of her. To her, we're still practically strangers."

"You know, Totsy, if you keep on the way you're headed, you may amount to something after all," he remarked abstractedly.

She waited for the catch in it, and there wasn't any. She thought of what she might say, and didn't dare. Well, look at my old man, she might have said, like a girl in a film, but the habit of distrusting his reaction was too strong. She smiled at him silently, though, and he smiled back in a preoccupied way.

"Advice to the lovelorn," he suggested, amiably enough. "Well, go on — what else?"

"I — can't think of anything else."

"You've told me what I did wrong. Now you're supposed to tell me how to do it right."

"Well, I — guess you should send her flowers — and take her to dinner where there's music — and talk about her books — "

"And propose regularly every hour on the hour," he took it up in a resigned singsong. "That way it could take forever."

"But you'll need some time, won't you, on account of the divorce?"

His eyes flickered and hardened, and she flinched instinctively at the change in him, which was bound to come if ever you said just what was in your mind.

"What do you know about the divorce?" he asked coldly.

"You — haven't got one, have you? That is — I understood — "

"You understood wrong."

"You — there is a divorce?" she faltered, the need for caution having been renewed.

"I assure you there is."

"But — I thought Margie said — "

"Margie doesn't — didn't know. It came too late. She wanted me to get one. She said it would close a door in my mind. But by the time I finally saw it her way and the lawyers managed to make contact and get the thing done — it didn't matter any more."

"But don't you see, it does matter now!" Joanna cried recklessly. "Margie was right! It's as though Margie *knew* about Eve."

He glanced at her obliquely, and away.

"Eve wouldn't care much for that idea," he said.

"We needn't mention it. Nobody else will." Joanna turned anxious eyes up the stairs. "I don't think she's packing — do you?"

"We ought to know soon." He lit another cigarette, nervously. "How long does it take a woman to pack?"

Joanna put her hands around her knees and hunched her shoulders as though a cold draft blew from somewhere.

"It's just a week-end bag. I was there when she took things out. But you know what? I don't think Margie will let her go."

Beau gave his daughter a suspicious look, and drew on the cigarette.

"What makes you say that?" he asked.

Joanna rested her chin on the top of her knees and shut her eyes.

"I like to pretend that Margie isn't really gone," she said very softly. "I like to think that she still looks after us here — and in that case — maybe she wants us to have Eve — in her place."

"It's possible," he said after a moment, and at his tone Joanna's eyes flew open, and she saw his face softened and smiling and rueful, and stretched out a hand to him across the stairs and felt his close on it, hard and warm.

XII

INSIDE the lilac room, Eve sat still with the door firmly closed, contemplating the situation into which she had deliberately walked.

With what she believed to be objective detachment she weighed the possibilities of avoiding another interview alone with her host, and knew that with half of Saturday and all of Sunday still to go, the chances were slim, even with Joanna on her side — and she realized now that Joanna was as determined in her way to involve her permanently in their lives as Marshall himself. *I used to pray that my father would marry again — I think you have worked some kind of miracle — to us it seems so inevitable* — that was Joanna. *For you I can do anything — don't let me go mad* — that was Joanna's father. One would need a heart of stone not to react. And there was no denying, he could be very attractive when he tried. Worth taking a lot of trouble over, yes; worth saving, surely. But hardly worth the rest of one's life, both of them put together!

She tried to survey her life impartially as it had been before Joanna's letter came — snug and solitary and insulated and busy. But what sort of living was it, really? No one would miss her daily if she wasn't there. No one depended on her for anything but the amenities. There was no one on whom she had any right to depend for more than the same.

You came home to an empty apartment — no one to say Hello, and What's new? and raise a welcoming tinkle with a cocktail shaker. You mixed yourself a drink and drank it alone, standing up in the kitchen, or you got on the phone for company, or you went out for same. Or if you'd had your head in the typewriter all day, nobody coming home to say I saw So-and-So, and How about a drink? Nobody across the way in a companionable silence during the evening, turning the pages of a book. Nobody who was automatically the other half of an invitation — you had to ring up and beg, borrow or steal an escort, or pretend you didn't mind going alone. No one to go round putting out lights and locking doors with himself inside, at the end of the day . . .

This was self-sufficiency. This was independence. This was career-woman stuff, and this was Eve Endicott, liking it up to now.

Tad had never unsettled her on it to any degree, and

Tad was right there with all the answers if she choose. Was it Richie then, with his odd, unhurried silences, his taciturn humor, his very knowing eyes, level under dark, level brows? But that was definitely Off, Richie was for Joanna, and no repining. So—there stood Beau Marshall again. *What a domestic scene*, he had said with a certain unpremeditated wistfulness. *Maybe Miss Endicott will have a civilizing influence in other ways as well*, he said. And so, judging by last evening, she had.

Eve allowed herself to contemplate the possibility, with a certain wistfulness of her own. A tea-table, a singing kettle, and the day closing in—herself, a pretty youngster like Joanna, a smiling, engaging, prosperous man who wanted her—a readymade civilized family unit. Something they needed as much as she did. Something she could give, and receive at the same time . . .

You're slipping, she told herself, into a sort of emotional blackmail. Sure they need you. Sure there's a case for adopting them and trying to help. But suppose you fail. Suppose he turns on you too, before long, and you begin to placate and to hedge, the way Joanna does. Suppose they pull you under, instead of your dragging them up. Well, you could always walk out on it, that has been done before. *He has been deserted once—twice would kill him. . . .*

And anyway—a kiss—I want you—stick around—Beau was playing it pretty safe. He had never given his wife a divorce, Richie said. Maybe Beau thought she didn't know that. Let us have no more of this Girl Scoutery. The man has driven himself nuts worshipping a woman who was always beyond his reach, until he made a fetich of his hopeless devotion. He was ripe for something odd and flagellant after his wife left him. He might have gone on the town with a chorus girl, or taken to serious drinking. Instead he got religion in the form of Margie Forrest — a kind of mental monastery. Who says Margie couldn't have handled it better if she tried?

Yes, there's that too, Eve thought. I would like to have one unbiased opinion of Margie — a nice catty woman's opinion, for choice, she thought with what was for her unusual cynicism. You get sort of fed up with Margie, around here, until heresy sets in, and you begin to wonder if she could have been some kind of sanctimonious blood-sucker who enjoyed having two strong men hog-tied. You could be burned at the stake in this house for suggesting such a thing. No, Richie loved her too, and Richie isn't mad. Perhaps this afternoon at Richie's house it would be possible to get some impression, first hand, of Richie's wife. Was she going to Richie's party with the Marshalls just as though nothing had happened, Eve queried herself. Certainly she was. What, she demanded of herself, was all this adolescent fuss about a kiss in a studio? So he made a pass at her. It had happened before, and please God she hadn't got past its happening again, sometime, somewhere.

She stood up and went to the mirror, and knew as she met her own eyes there that what took place in the studio could not be dismissed as easily as that. For the first time in her acquaintance with Marshall she had felt a twinge of the fear he inspired in other people. But he wasn't trying to scare her then. She was immune to that. It was his good behavior that had bred in her a sudden uneasiness pointing to panic. Because when he was like that one's guard went down, watchfulness seemed treachery, the charm worked, the spell was cast — one forgot, one did not want to remember, that he was ever otherwise. He was much more dangerous when he seemed at his best. Always remember that, she admonished herself sagely, picking up her lipstick. Always remember to run when things begin to shimmer and you feel yourself slipping. . . .

His lightning changes of mood were something she could neither comprehend nor condone. Even-tempered herself, with a natural optimism, she took a certain pride in her own equanimity and had little sympathy, however much outward patience, with people who succumbed to blues and megrims and grouches. But here was a man with a demon, a man who might have been a good companion, witty, worldly, even lovable . . .

The hand which held the lipstick paused suspended,

as something turned over in her mind with a small satisfied click, like a combination lock which had been solved. The thing to do next was to get behind Beau's moods to their source and origin. His wife had left him, presumably because he was impossible to live with. But did anybody *know* that? Was he the same before she went? And even if he was, could he perhaps have had a reason? Joanna said she remembered her mother. But she had never said that she loved her, or missed her when she had gone. Surely that was rather odd. Joanna was old enough to have had an opinion, when her mother went away.

The lipstick traced its careful course, while Eve contemplated the Marshalls in a new light. Nobody said anything about Beau's wife except Richie, who had hardly known her. Beau was in a way on trial for his life, and in a trial you called witnesses. The missing witness was his wife. There were only two people, so far as Eve knew, who could answer questions about his wife. And they were both in this house.

She passed a powder puff over her face, walked to the door, opened it briskly, and came to the top of the stairs.

They were still sitting there together, and their two welcoming faces turned up to her in touching unison. She paused, looking down at them with reluctant affection while they rose and stood, one against either bannister, with room for her between. A couple of psychopaths, were they, as Tad had said, or just a pair of lost souls who only needed a lamp in the window?

"Totsy has pointed out to me that I may not have made myself clear," he was saying, with one hand held out to her. "I neglected to state that my intentions are honorable. Will you marry me, Eve?"

Her eyes went from one to the other incredulously. She was flabbergasted that he could pick it up again like this, in front of Joanna — that he and Joanna seemed suddenly on a new and intimate footing — that he was even in a position to offer marriage with such confidence —

"You really are the most *fantastic* people," she got out.

"What's the matter now?" he queried in apparent chagrin. "Aren't you kind of hard to please? You didn't like it the other way."

"Father, we mustn't rush her." Joanna ran up the steps and laid motherly arms around Eve. "She hardly knows us, after all! It's not fair to ask her to decide so soon!"

"Are you sure we improve with acquaintance?" he asked with disarming irony.

"It's all right, Eve, he's got the divorce," Joanna reassured her. "Margie made him get it. I didn't know that. I guess nobody did."

Eve looked past her gravely, and Marshall gave back an honest stare.

"It's on the records," he said. "I can prove it. I admit

I was slow, but there were difficulties. It came through only last December. Should I send out cards?"

"Everybody's going to be awfully surprised," Joanna remarked with satisfaction. "I was."

"Now that it's come up, I suppose it might make a difference," he said to Eve, and real anxiety showed through the bantering tone.

"Well — yes, I suppose it might," she admitted, and allowed herself to be drawn down the stairs towards him, captive in the loving circle of Joanna's arm.

"If we are going to have cocktails before lunch, and I for one am in favor of it," he suggested, joining them on her other side as they moved towards the drawing-room, "it is time that somebody went out in the kitchen and did something practical about ice and glasses and bottles on a tray."

"All right," said Joanna happily. "I will." And she left them.

He closed the drawing-room door behind himself and Eve, and stood smiling at her with his back against it, relaxed, confident, possessive.

"I got carried away," he confessed with a capitalized sweetness and reason. "Don't forget — the effect you have on me is still a new sensation."

She put up one hand against him as he came towards her.

"Beau, I'd like to ask a question. If you don't want to

answer it you needn't — and we'll just have a cocktail and eat lunch like civilized people."

"Let me guess. You are going to ask if I have tried psychiatry," he said, unabashed. "Everyone does, sooner or later."

"No. I hadn't even thought of it. I'll ask my own question, please — though it may make you angry."

"You have a right to ask me anything you want to," he said simply.

"Very well, then. What was your wife like?"

He stood quite still while his eyes widened on her face. She watched minutely for his change of mood. There was no anger, no secretiveness, no refusal in his steady blue gaze. She sought the right word for it, with her writer's exactitude in words. Admiration was there, and wonderment — and a sort of gratification, as though she had justified and surpassed his expectations. Then, holding the silence, he moved away from her to the table, turning his back, reaching for a cigarette and a lighter.

"O.K.," she said kindly at last. "We'll just eat lunch."

"Wait, wait, I'm going to answer!" His smile was easy and genuine, his cigarette was alight. "But you've put it in a very difficult form, it's caught me flat-footed. Not — Why did she leave me? or What broke up our marriage? Not any of the easy ones. Not you! You ask — *What was she like?* I could be fancy and say, Like quicksilver. Or I could be coarse and say, Like a pain in the neck. But

I would like to be truthful. That takes time." Carrying the cigarette, he wandered to the window and looked out blindly at the sunny day. "Did you ever come down stairs in the dark and think you had arrived at the bottom and then there was one more step? Chances are, you break your neck. Cerise was like that." He glanced at her sidewise. "Doesn't help? I'll try again. Joanna is not my child."

Eve made a sort of sound. It was wordless.

"By the look on your foolish face, you don't seem to follow me, so I'll put it another way," he said. "I am not Joanna's father, though Cerise was her mother. Got it?"

Again he waited for her to speak. "You asked me what my wife was like. I've told you. But it's something that I have never told anyone but you. Do you understand that?"

She nodded slowly. He meant her to understand that even Margie had not known — and that he had made that difference between them. She swallowed, trying to find her voice.

"The father?" she asked.

"Dead, long ago. Smashed himself up in a car. Drunk at the time, no doubt. That's what *he* was like."

"Oh, Beau, I don't know what to s-say — "

"Next question?" he prompted, and his smile was whimsical — charming.

"Yes, I've got more questions! How did it happen? I mean — "

"That's a silly one! You're a big girl now, Eve — "

"I meant — could you be quite sure — ?"

"You meant, did I see or hear. I did. Like a French farce. Even then, I had to laugh. It was all there — a lot of extra doors, and people scampering around in the dark — " He paused because she had made, involuntarily, a small fastidious face. "There was even a simple matter of arithmetic," he added briefly.

"But — was she married to you at the time?"

"She was. It was all pretty tiresome. Shall I go on?"

"If you — yes, please."

"She was half French. I don't know why I bring that in, it doesn't explain anything but her name. We were students together — art students have a lot of fun, and we were all frightfully Bohemian and cute — Greenwich Village at its corniest. I was only playing at it — to me she was the real thing, living in a garret, starving, modelling to get money enough to eat and pay the rent. So we got married and set up very picturesque housekeeping together in fairly sanitary surroundings. I expected the same old friends to go on running in and out — I even expected to go on supporting some of them as usual — so it was quite a while before I began to catch on. Not that it made much difference after I did, except that then we had bigger and better rows. You mustn't assume that

Joanna was the result of just one small amateur indiscretion of my wife's."

"But — after you came here, surely she — "

"By the time we came here we had reached an understanding of sorts. You see, I always had money, and that's very important to a woman like Cerise. We had agreed to cover up on Joanna and raise her as my daughter. Fortunately she looked like her mother, and Cerise never looked at all like the kind of person she really was."

"If you had ever let anyone have any idea — "

"You aren't a man, or you couldn't say that. By the time we came here my whole life was a frenzied effort to prove to the world and myself and Cerise and Joanna that I was the master of my household and the father of my wife's child. I don't expect you to understand why it was so important to me, but believe me, it was. There were no more children, you see. There couldn't be. I suppose that came into it too."

"And then — in spite of your trouble to hold things together — she went away after all."

"She didn't go, she was pushed," he said with a snap. "Joanna was getting old enough to notice things. I couldn't have that. I threw them out. I was thinking of Joanna, because by then I almost believed she was mine."

"Oh, Beau, the truth would have made such a difference — "

"Don't you realize, I meant it to die with me?" He put

out the cigarette and came and took her hands in his. "You are the first thing I have ever wanted more than the illusion I had built up around Joanna. Not even Margie ever cracked that shell."

"If you had told her — "

"She never asked me. She left that for you."

The door-knob turned awkwardly — things rattled on the tray as Joanna edged her way through the narrow opening, both hands occupied, her soft, fair hair swinging on her cheeks. Beau dropped Eve's hands and spun round towards the door.

"*Oh, God,* Joanna, can't you ever take a *hint?*"

She halted in her tracks, holding the heavy tray, at a total loss.

"You s-said you wanted cocktails — "

"I do!" he moaned, and went to take the tray from her with something like courtesy. "You leave me no choice, you pitiless angel of mercy — I do indeed want a drink!"

xiii

UNFORTUNATELY, no guests had been invited to lunch that day, which might have relieved the situation. Fortified by an unaccustomed two cocktails, Eve took her place at table in the sunny dining-room — noticing again what a nice house it was, and what a luxurious one. Cerise, adrift with somebody who earned a chauffeur's wages, must have looked back more than once.

Again it was Joanna who kept the talk going, in her innocent mothering of what she hoped was romance, and Eve was grateful for her chatter about the garden and the birds who were nesting there, and the care of flowering plants, in which Joanna had made herself something of an expert. She spoke of flower-shows and flower arrangements, and what had taken first prize, and the merits of bird-houses and feeders and what to put out for attractive bird food — she had picked up a baby bluebird once, she told them, and hoped to raise it, but it had lain in cold, rain-soaked grass all night and soon died. She had a whole shelf of bird books and could identify most of what she saw. Birds were company, she explained. A canary would be company indoors too, but Father said they always screeched. Eve denied that canaries had to screech, and made a mental note to see that Joanna got one to keep, as soon as possible.

Beau said little during the meal, attending to his food and allowing the conversation to roll over him. He was not sulking, and his silence put no damper on the other two. He seemed merely a little absent-minded — and hungry.

By the time they rose from the table Eve and Joanna had decided on a tour outside, and Joanna conscientiously invited him to join them. He had already turned away towards the studio, and he glanced back with a cheerful wave of his hand in dismissal.

"I've seen the garden," he said. "You go along with Mar — I mean Eve while I finish a sketch." If he had not corrected himself, if he had slid off the first syllable into "Ma-Eve" the slip would hardly have been noticeable. As it was, silence fell like a brick, and it was he who recovered first. "Sorry," he said with a quite spontaneous smile. "Sheer habit. It's a compliment, really." And the studio door closed behind him.

Joanna slid her arm through Eve's and they went out

through the French windows into a flawless spring day.

"It *was* habit," Joanna said with some constraint. "I've heard him say that a thousand times — 'You go along with Margie — ' and then we'd see him looking out from the studio. Not spying, I don't mean, just as though he liked to see us there together. You don't mind, do you?" she added anxiously, looking into Eve's face.

"Well, I don't think I'm flattered," Eve said gropingly.

"You should be — it just *shows* how you belong here, doesn't it!"

Eve made no reply, and they paced on slowly across the grass, rather conscious of the studio windows behind them. Joanna's garden was a beautiful sunny oblong, with a central lawn and deep flower-borders on three sides, overhung by a couple of ample trees with white lawn furniture in their shade. Arm in arm, they ambled along the side where the tulips bloomed, and Joanna recited their names, which to Eve were singularly lovely. When they reached the end farthest from the house Eve went to a bench which encircled a tree-trunk and they sat down, while a companionable pause descended over them. She felt that Joanna was awaiting an announcement of some kind, and all she had was more questions.

"I was wondering," she began quietly without leading up to it, "what you felt about your mother."

"You mean, when she went away?" Joanna instantly froze into a wary stillness.

"Well, even before that. Did she watch birds with you, and work in the garden?"

"Oh, no, she didn't care about things like that." The denial was prompt and unpremeditated.

"What did she care about?"

"I don't know — clothes, maybe — and dancing — having a good time."

"Did they go out a lot?"

"Quite a lot."

"Who looked after you?"

"I had a nice nurse for a while. And then a sort of governess who gave me lessons — she left in a huff, I don't know what happened. There was always a cook who lived in, in those days. None of them stayed very long. After Mother went away there was another governess, and then Father said I was old enough to do up my own buttons and go to school."

"Wasn't that better? Did you like school?"

"I thought I would, but it didn't work out very well. It was a day school in Scottville, about twelve miles from here. Father drove me over every morning, and Miss Delafield — she was one of the teachers — drove a bit out of her way to bring me home. They had some sort of arrangement."

"Why didn't it work out?"

"Everything was so different for the other girls. That is, they had both fathers and mothers, except one or two, and they thought it very odd that instead of doing something respectable like Wall Street, my father was home all day painting, and that I liked it that way — because of course I said I did. They had dogs, and brothers and sisters, and played games, and gave parties — I was always out of step, with things like that. So I was really glad when it was over — when I graduated and could stay home. Some of the mothers tried to be kind to me — but I never knew what to talk about. I could always talk to Margie, though. Once I had her, the rest didn't matter."

"Didn't you miss your mother, when she had gone?"

"No, not really. You see, I never knew her very well."

"Never — ?" Eve prompted, sitting very still for fear this fountain of information should dry up.

"She was away so much of the time anyway — it seemed as though she was always just getting back from somewhere or just setting out. I expect Father gave her too much money to spend. She'd take the car and the driver and go to the city for the day — and then she'd think of something else to do and not come back for several more days. Father didn't seem to mind her being away so much as he minded the bills. They used to have awful rows about the bills, and Father would threaten to fire Albert."

"Albert?"

"He was the chauffeur. She wouldn't learn to drive the

car herself, and that kept Albert hanging about in town instead of living here in his quarters over the garage as he was supposed to. Father thought he took advantage — used the car when she didn't know, and things like that. I hated Albert. He patronized me, or else talked to me as though I was a dog. A child always hates to be treated differently from grown-ups. It was Albert she went away with, finally — I never could see why. Father may be hard to get along with, but at least he's — well, bad as it is sometimes with Father, I'm thankful Mother didn't like me well enough to take me with her. I never could have stood Albert."

"Didn't *like* you?" Eve murmured.

"No, I don't think she did. Not the way mothers usually do. She liked to dress me up so I looked cute. But with her I always felt like a doll, as though I could be put down and left whenever she got tired of me. And that's just what she did, in the end. With Father it was too much the other way. I think he was jealous even of Margie. She said it was because he was lonely, but I don't know — perhaps it was the other way round, and he was jealous of Margie's spending time with me."

"Did you see quite a lot of her?"

"All I could manage to. Without Margie I'd have had a lot of wrong ideas. When I was little I used to try to pretend that she was my real mother, but it wasn't much good — I *knew* about mine, and about Albert, I couldn't really forget them. I'd hate to think what I might have turned into, if it hadn't been for Margie. And Richie too, of course, you couldn't think of them separately before she died. I don't know how he lived through that, I honestly don't."

"People do," Eve said thoughtfully, remembering the Battle of the Bulge and the telegram. "You find something to go on with somehow — and finally, almost without your realizing it, the worst is over. That's all you can hope for — to survive the worst. After that you stand an even chance."

Joanna sighed.

"Poor Richie. Being a man, and so sensible and grown up and all, I suppose he'd never think to play my game."

"Your game? What is that?" Eve turned a searching look on the saddened young face beside her.

"I've never told anybody, except I happened to mention it to Father today and he said — " Joanna's hand went guiltily to her mouth and she left the sentence unfinished.

"What game?" Eve insisted.

"He said you wouldn't care for it."

"Why wouldn't I? Tell me what it is."

"Well, I — " Joanna looked away from her, down the lawn where robins ran, questing for worms. "I like to pretend that Margie is still somewhere near — can still see and hear us, and maybe tell us what to do, if we listen hard enough. I have a feeling we can keep Margie here, if we try."

"You mustn't do that." Eve spoke more sharply than she knew. "That's not the way to look at death. You must let them go. I don't mean forget them — but to cling on to them and try to communicate with them and live with them still — especially in a young person like you, that's all wrong. You must learn to do without them, or put something in their place — "

"I suppose so," said Joanna softly. "And that's why I'm so grateful for you. But you don't mind, do you, if I go on believing that Margie made me write that letter to you — so I would have something to put in her place?"

"Yes, I do mind," Eve replied vigorously. "Lots of people write letters to me without any prompting from the spirit world. You liked my books and you were lonely, so you wrote. Have you any idea how many people do that — total strangers, just as you were?"

"I suppose dozens do," Joanna conceded unwillingly. "All the same — ask anybody — you're very like her."

"That's got nothing to do with it. I was just as much like her before she died as I am now. She must have been about the same age — and I wasn't just an empty body going round waiting for her to die and take possession."

"Oh, no, of course I didn't mean — I only thought she

might have sent you to us because you *were* so like her — "

"I wasn't sent, I came — at some trouble to myself," Eve insisted with what she recognized as unnecessary heat. "I'm not stooging for Margie here, I stuck my nose in because I wanted to help. Maybe I should have minded my own business."

Joanna sat silent and drooping beside her on the bench, and Eve felt compunction. No sense in taking Joanna's head off just because she was indulging in a bit of amateur spiritualism. She laid a quick hand on Joanna's, which turned in her clasp confidingly.

"I didn't mean to snap at you, darling," Eve said. "But I do think this Margie business has got a bit out of hand. I know you all loved her very much, but if she was all you say she was she'd hate to be turned into a sort of cult."

"Please don't be jealous of her." Joanna raised brimming eyes to Eve's face. "Please believe we're only grateful to you for wanting to help."

Eve gazed back at her speechlessly. Perhaps it did sound as though she was jealous of Margie, when she was merely impatient of their obsession. Or it might be that she felt a hovering presence too strongly for her own comfort, and so it was against her own imagination, as much as Joanna's, that she hit out. Because right here and now, under a blue sky in mid-afternoon, it seemed to her that she and Joanna were but two out of three — that they were overheard — and that she spoke as much to the other one as to Joanna.

"Richie wouldn't like it either," she said severely. "You said yourself that it would never occur to him to play any such game."

"No," Joanna agreed with her pathetic docility. "Richie would say I was being spooky, I expect. Except — you never can be sure what Richie really thinks," she added with a sort of pride that this was so. "At least, I suppose Margie could. I can't."

"Getting back to your mother," said Eve, for she had had enough of Margie again, "what finally happened, do you know? Was there a row before she left?"

"There were always rows," Joanna said wearily. "Father wasn't easy to live with, even then. I don't know which of them was more to blame, if that's what you mean. Sometimes they didn't speak to each other for days. When she did go it was very sudden, I think — she didn't even say good-bye to me. One day she was gone, and he said she wasn't coming back. I wondered why he minded so much. I didn't."

Joanna hadn't noticed anything, then, Eve thought with some relief. It was doubtless better for her to remain puzzled and uncertain, even resentful, about the circumstances of her mother's departure — Beau had spared her something, after all. Up to a point Beau had done so well by Joanna, there was no sense in the way he mucked it up in other directions. He could have done so much better so easily. He had provided the basic security a child needs — magnanimously, if you like — he had endured a good deal to preserve a more than comfortable background for her, he had protected her from disillusionment or shock in what had become an impossible situation. And then he had isolated, bullied, and humiliated her in his own way. Apparently every time he looked at her he saw Cerise — apparently he thought his methods with the child would eliminate heredity — or possibly, as Eve had said once before, he was simply taking it out on Joanna.

"Did they get along all right before Albert came?" she asked, piecing the thing together like a story-plot.

"They never got along, I guess. Albert was only here about a year. In fact, I think Albert was mostly an innocent bystander."

Eve stared at her.

"You mean she wasn't in love with him?"

"He was the chauffeur," Joanna explained patiently. "He was bad-tempered and common, even I could see that. Handsome in a movie hero sort of way, but — well, not very *clean*, I thought. Of course it was a long time ago, but I've thought a lot about it. He hadn't any money, and she was a very expensive person. I can't imagine her *staying* with Albert, even though they left here together. He couldn't afford her."

"Do you have any idea where she is now?"

"No. Sometimes I wonder about it."

"Would you like to see her again?"

"I don't think so. I never knew her very well," Joanna repeated. "At least Father knew how to get along with a child, when I was little — he talked sensibly to me, and remembered my birthdays and drove me to school and — Isn't it funny," said Joanna, "as soon as you start to count up, Father sounds all right. I oughtn't to complain about him, it's just the *way* he does things — he *over*does things, I guess. But it can't have been much fun for him, can it, all these years. Margie said a funny thing once. She said when Father found out there wasn't any Santa Claus he slammed the door forever on Christmas."

"I see what she meant," Eve said reluctantly. "Joanna, there is one great difference between you and your father which is very important. For you, it is only a game to pretend that Margie isn't dead. It's a thing you do deliberately, knowing that you do it — isn't that what you meant to tell me?"

Joanna nodded doubtfully.

"I knew he'd give himself away sooner or later," she said with a sigh. "I wasn't sure how. It happened when he called you Margie by mistake, didn't it. You knew then if you didn't before. It's not a game with him, I know. He can't help it. He can't stop. I guess I was hoping you wouldn't notice or — that you could cure him of it almost overnight, so that you were *you* to him, and not Margie."

Eve sat very still, pitched her voice very low.

"He only wants to put me in her place — to shut his eyes and have Margie after all. Isn't that it?"

"It's because you're so like her," Joanna offered as an excuse. "But you will stand by us, Eve?" she pleaded. "Maybe, between us, we can pull him out of it. He's so much better since you came. He's not mad, Eve — not yet. Please give us a chance," she said, and hid her face against Eve's shoulder.

Eve put an arm around her inconspicuously and said against the soft hair, "He can see us from the windows — " and Joanna's head came up with a jerk.

"I didn't mean to corner you," she said. "I'm worse than he is."

Eve shook her head with a smile.

"Not so long as you can say so," she said.

xiv

THERE was nothing special about Margie's house, Eve discovered that afternoon at tea time. It was in excellent but standard *Country Life* taste, well lived in. Whoever looked after it now was a good housekeeper, doubtless trained by Margie herself. Its polished wood surfaces shone discreetly dustless, the chintzes and curtains were fresh, the comfortable accumulation of loose books and recent magazines was not too much regimented into unread tidiness. Her first comprehensive glance around caught a large silver frame on the grand piano, and she guessed that the portrait it contained must be of Margie. If they moved it before Richie's sister-in-law started to play, there might be a chance to look at it more closely. In spite of its presence, there was not the same feeling here of something that lingered and hovered as there was in Beau's house. Perhaps, she thought with real relief, there is no reason here for haunting. Here is acceptance and release. Richie has let her go. . . .

A tea-table was laid with silver and china, but it was early yet. Stella had all the usual complimentary things to say about Eve's books, with no suspicion of having boned up because of the meeting, and Eve noticed that her latest volume lay inconspicuously on an end-table by the hearth. Richie's home-work, she thought affectionately, and wondered what he thought of that one.

She watched the two men warily, because of Joanna's remark that her father hated Richie for Margie's death. Nothing was visible on the surface today but the most casual, good-humored tolerance. Beau was on his best behavior still, and every time she glanced his way she got an impression that he was awaiting her appreciation of that supremely funny fact. A conscious, conscientious virtue pervaded him. He was being good naughtily, the way a mischievous child is good, not just by breathing, but by a deliberate effort of will, an effort which automatically required recognition, even congratulation. But inevitably both she and Joanna relaxed, basked in his sunny mood, and by the time the maid brought in sandwiches and cakes and lighted the spirit-lamp under the silver kettle they had begun to enjoy themselves.

Richie rose when the tea arrived, and standing with a casual hand on the back of the chair behind the tea-pot he invited Joanna to pour out for them. It was nicely done, whether designed to elevate her to grown up status among grown ups, or to gratify the pride of a youngster among them. Conversation flowed on with no one seeming to attach any significance to Joanna's position — Stella and Jerome had more than once seen her pour the tea under Margie's smiling guidance, for it was from Margie that she had learned all the graces, first by example and then by supervised performance.

But as Joanna sat down diffidently behind a service similar to the one she handled quite competently at home, a warning bell rang in Eve's mind — wasn't this neighborly gesture on Richie's part the sort of thing Joanna's father referred to as enlarging her ego? As long as Beau remained absorbed in Stella Forrest, Eve refrained from noticing him. But she felt tension resume in Joanna and her own nerves began to crisp at the edges.

Joanna got through the first round with no comment from Beau, though her hands were unsteady as they moved over the china. Richie acted as butler, handing the cups as she filled them, and the food. Eve drew a cautious breath. If they survived this afternoon without complications, Beau Marshall had really reformed.

At that moment he rose and walked to the tea-table to set down his empty cup. Pausing there, he ran a cold, ironical eye over Joanna, who returned his gaze helplessly from behind the silver.

"Congratulations," he said, and his teeth showed on the word. "For a dress rehearsal, I must say that went very well."

Eve heard a murmur beside her, where Richie's brother Jerome sat. "Here we go again," it said.

"Beau, will you take my cup, please?" That was Stella, in an instinctive attempt to head him off, though her cup had just been refilled.

"Why, certainly." He looked down at it, still in her hand. "But you haven't finished."

"I've had enough, thanks. Didn't really want a second cup."

"Is it cold?"

"No — oh, no. Just set it down, will you?"

He took it from her and returned to the table.

"Make Stella a fresh cup," he said to Joanna. "This one isn't up to the usual standard."

Stella and Jerome exchanged glances. Richie stabbed out his cigarette in an ashtray, but sat still.

"It's lovely tea," Eve said, willing to sound banal in the effort to remind Beau of her presence and the advisability of his continuing to behave well. "Earl Grey, isn't it? I used to bring it back from England before the war."

"You always get Earl Grey in this house," said Marshall, standing over Joanna waiting for Stella's cup, which chattered in its saucer as she handed it to him.

"There has been no substitution in the tea — so far. Doubtless we shall soon be asked to accept a poor imitation of that as well as of the dispenser of it."

"That was uncalled for," Richie remarked quietly.

"On the contrary, I think it was decidedly in order," Marshall insisted, as Stella received the fresh cup from his hand and set it down on the end-table beside her to ignore. "I had no idea that Joanna would be promoted so fast."

"Oh, please, Father, Richie had no idea of — I never dreamed — "

"You can both tell that to the Marines," said Marshall rudely. The glitter was in his eyes again, his lips were drawn in his rigid closed smile.

Eve saw the storm signals with chagrin and despair. He had not been able to keep it up, as she might have known he wouldn't. *For you I can do anything* — yes, for less than one day. She knew by the bitterness of her disappointment in him that her imagination, at least, had been caught by the idea of undertaking the rescue of Beau Marshall along with his daughter.

"I was promised some music this afternoon," she said a little too markedly, and caught Stella's eyes.

"Hark at Eve, being tactful and trying to preserve the decencies," Marshall remarked, and the bright blue stare shifted to rest on her. "No doubt this is the kind of thing you would recommend as the happy ending for

Joanna, Miss Endicott? That she should step into a dead woman's shoes?"

"Behave yourself, Beau." Eve felt herself trembling. Richie rose from his chair, and she checked him with a quick, imperative hand. Stella went to the piano and ran her fingers over the keys as though in reply to Eve's suggestion that she play. The sound drew Marshall's gaze in that direction, and it fell on the framed portrait of Margie enthroned there.

"She would never allow the piano to be played while it was cluttered up with things on top," he said, and moved to the piano and picked up the frame, sweeping a silk scarf off the lid with his other hand at the same time, so that a small ashtray clattered off on to the polished wood. "There doesn't seem to be much point in keeping this around, does there?" he said, holding the picture so that it faced the room. "Or shall we just turn it to the wall?"

"Put it down, Beau," Richie said in a low voice.

"The Queen is dead," Marshall went on heedlessly, and laughed. "Long live the Queen!"

"I said, Put it down." Richie started towards him, and again Eve threw a quick hand on to his sleeve. Her fingers had to tighten and grip to hold him there. She hated scenes, and her heart was beating somewhere up at the top of her head. Yet somehow it was up to her to put an end to this one, and enable them all to emerge from it with some kind of dignity and self-respect. It was up to her to write herself some pretty well-turned lines, and quick.

"I never knew the woman you call Margie," she said clearly into the tense silence which paralyzed them all. "I only know that she was greatly loved by all of you. Until now, I hadn't even any idea how she looked." She crossed the floor deliberately and took the heavy silver frame from Beau's hand and stood holding it between both hers, looking down at it. She saw a sensitive, beautiful face with no real resemblance to her own, as they had said — except in a sort of over-all expression lurking in the tenderly curved mouth and direct gaze. She saw, what's more, some justification for the legend of Margie — the face in the photograph showed no sign of phony piety or selfish prettiness. It had the pure, almost impersonal beauty of a saint. "As I understand it, Margie was some kind of genius who succeeded in running this menagerie with a minimum of bloodshed — not a job I can envy her," Eve continued after a moment and looked straight into Marshall's face as she set the silver frame on a table near the piano. "I came here today for the first time, almost a stranger. I wasn't involved in the life that went on here, I'm a very recent onlooker. More than once I have found myself wondering exactly how I got here, and why. I'm not psychic as a rule — but it occurred to me while Joanna poured the tea that Margie herself might have chosen and taught her successor — that perhaps Richie was not acting on a random impulse just now, he was following a design which was imprinted on this room by Margie, before she left it." She looked round at them, one by one — Richie last. "Perhaps that's why I'm here — perhaps because somebody had to come and say that." She wrenched her gaze from Richie's and turned away towards Stella, who still sat at the keyboard. "That was Chopin you started to play, wasn't it? I can't think of anything I'd rather hear."

The music began softly, competently, swelled, and possessed the room. Eve dropped limply into the nearest chair and fixed her eyes on her cold, trembling hands in her lap. But she still saw Richie's face, and its expression of incredulous, enigmatic dismay. She had needed words — lines — and because she was practiced in words the little speech had come, from her own experience in turning a climax, or from the surcharged air — or from Margie. She had headed off the scene, got the music going, won everybody a chance to breathe and cool off. Joanna sat motionless, crouched in the chair behind the tea-table, her white face almost hidden by the forward-swinging hair. Beau was hiding behind the useful cigarette stage-business. Neither Richie nor Jerome seemed to breathe, much less move.

She had played Richie's hand for him, she realized.

Even, she had thrown Joanna at his head. Staring down at her clammy fingers, with the Nocturne falling on eardrums which were already ringing with her own furious blood, she wondered — *was she wrong?*

XV

THEY walked home at twilight almost in silence, the brilliant, healing music still lingering around them. In the hall Marshall said in a perfectly ordinary voice, "How about a drink before going up to change?"

"Not now, thank you." Eve continued her way towards the stairs without a glance in his direction.

She was aware that Joanna came up behind her, but they parted at the door of the lilac room with only a rueful smile exchanged.

Eve was angry through and through. Angry with herself for ever contemplating the quixotic project of saving Marshall from himself, and for allowing him to glimpse the fact that she had done so — angry with him for leading her into it, unspeakably angry that he had then let her down before everybody. She was even angry with Richie, for if he had left the pouring out to Stella, which was surely the usual thing to do, the crisis would not have occurred. Unless, as she had been somehow inspired to suggest at the time, Richie had truly acted under some mysterious compulsion . . .

Things had reached a point now where it seemed to Eve not impossible to suppose that after years of devoted effort to reconcile her little world, when Margie had to leave her task unfinished she could still strive to guide and protect the people she had loved. And if you once conceded to Margie the power of some occult action, then the whole thing fitted in with Joanna's childish game — the fantastic letter to a stranger, the *right* stranger, who would be sure to respond — who having responded could be enticed step by step further into the coils — who would react like Margie herself, think like Margie, sound like Margie, *become* Margie in their obsessed minds. Coincidence? Was *anything* coincidence? *She promised me there was someone like you.* . . . And what had Margie promised Richie?

Eve shivered and glanced round the darkening room defensively. You're as bad as the rest of them, she told herself severely. You know perfectly well you undertook this thing of your own free will, against good advice. You asked for it, and you got it. You meddled. Me fix. Can't you *learn?* You started it, and therefore you can quit, any time you like — can't you. These people are nothing to you. A month ago you'd never heard of any of them. A month hence it won't matter to you any more. They have no claim, no hold on you — except what you have given them. You aren't psychic at all, that was just a good line. Margie can't turn your life around, Margie is dead and gone, it's all in their minds. . . .

A chilly wind had come up at sundown. It blew the white ruffled curtain in across the dressing-table where Joanna had put yellow daffodils in a tall slim vase. The flowers caught the edge of the curtain and the vase tipped over with a crash on the glass top of the table.

Eve leaped for the bag on the luggage-rack and flung it open and began to empty the bureau drawers into it. Her hands were shaking with something more than haste.

There was a soft knocking on the door. Beau again, come to apologize again? She made no reply, but the sound of a bureau drawer closing was audible through the door.

"Please, Eve — may I come in?" It was Joanna.

With a bursting repentance Eve realized that she was not being fair to Joanna. She herself could walk out on Beau Marshall if she chose. It wasn't as easy as that for Joanna.

"Come in, my dear!" she called, trying to sound cordial and casual.

Joanna had gone to her own room and shut the door when she left Eve a little while before. It was her private place, always scrupulously respected by her father, who never intruded there. She sat down on the first thing she came to — the bench in front of the dressing-table — and remained motionless, staring at the carpet, thinking things out.

The scene in Richie's drawing-room had shocked her more than anything Beau had ever done before. She was still sick and cold with shame and pity for him, convinced at last that they couldn't save him. With Eve in the same room, he still preferred Margie, the disembodied idea of Margie, to flesh and blood. And now Eve would probably never try again.

Loving Eve as she had come to do, Joanna was suddenly anxious to see her free of this frightening entanglement with Margie's memory. It wouldn't do. They had no right. Eve had come into their lives like an unwary fly into a spider's web. Now Joanna only wanted to cut her loose and see her safely away. It was not Eve's destined obligation, she was not a Marshall, and this was a Marshall matter.

Philosophically, with more resignation than despair, Joanna accepted her own dreary future. The dream of escape was over, the foolish, enchanted dream which had begun with Eve's books and would go with Eve — because Eve must go now, and Richie too.

Joanna had read Richie's face when Eve made her disastrous little speech — and had seen more plainly than anyone else, because she knew him better, that he was surprised and embarrassed and — floored, by Eve's suggestion that Margie had set the pattern for that afternoon. Joanna could see that so far from being his intention, such a thing had never occurred to him. She wondered how she could convey to him now that she understood about that, and he needn't try to spare her feelings. It seemed to Joanna that she had no feelings any more — just numbness. She hoped it lasted that way.

So there was no longer any point in the comforting game that Margie still watched over them, or had anything to do with writing the letter to Eve, now that nothing would come of it. Except for Richie. In a roundabout sort of way, the letter had given Eve to Richie. Perhaps, if Margie had intended anything at all, it was that. And all that was left was just what she had started with — the difficult, unhappy, demented man who had shut himself up in the studio alone with his obsession.

Joanna stirred and glanced round her in the fading light. Cocktails — dinner — and an evening without guests — how on earth were they to get through all that now. Luncheon had been bad enough. Perhaps Eve should get away before something more broke loose. Perhaps this time she really was packing. Joanna rose, feeling a bit giddy and very tired. She had better go and tell Eve that she saw it wasn't any use, and thank her for trying to help. . . .

She opened Eve's door slowly and went in, and closed it behind her, leaning against it while she took in Eve's haphazard start at packing.

"He was afraid you'd do that this morning," was all she could think of to say at first. "When we were sitting on the stairs."

"If he thinks I'm going to let him off again he has another guess coming. That was it. I'm all through."

"Poor Richie, he never should have done it," Joanna said tenderly. "It was like the sherry. He forgot Margie wasn't there. He didn't think how it might look."

"It must have looked all right to him."

"Well, you see, I'd poured the tea before, when Margie asked me to. But to Father it only meant that Margie wasn't there any more. You can see how it was."

"I saw."

"You were wonderful, Eve. *I* couldn't think of anything to stop him." Joanna came away from the door and bent to pick up a stocking which had fallen to the floor, made it into a tidy little ball and tucked it into the open bag.

"I suppose I sounded just like Margie again!" Eve snapped, having spilled her face-powder in her ill-organized hurry. "I know, it's a compliment!" she added as Joanna opened her mouth. "And I can feel her even here, right now, trying to tell me what to do, trying to pin me down! I'm going to get away from Margie, now, tonight, before anything else happens! I feel like a ouija-board as it is!"

"There isn't a train till nine-thirty," Joanna said unargumentatively.

"I'll wait at the station. What do I do about getting a cab?"

"I've been thinking. You'd better run over and ask Richie to drive you to the station. Then you won't have to use our telephone. There's an extension in the studio. Sometimes he listens in."

"Did he send you here to keep tabs on me?"

"No. That was this morning. As a matter of fact, I came because I was afraid you might not be planning to go."

"Give me that again?" Eve paused with a folded dress in her hands.

"I've just suddenly realized you mustn't get caught here like me. Oh, I know I tried to catch you myself in the beginning. But I can see now that we were both clutching on to you like drowning people, Father and I, and that we have no right to cannibalize your life to save ourselves."

"You're saved, all right," Eve said bluntly. "You can count on Richie now to get you out of it. What I'm not prepared to do is put up with your father the way Margie did."

"She always had Richie, so it didn't matter. When you're alone it's not so good."

"You aren't alone any longer, you're coming to New York with me tonight. Plenty of room at the apartment. We'll do the town and forget all of this." When Joanna made no reply Eve turned to look at her. "*Now* what?" she asked patiently.

"I've been acting like a baby," Joanna said, not meeting her eyes. "I thought at first that if I could only get you to stay here and look after Father I'd be free. But it couldn't work out that way. I don't think that was what Margie meant after all." Joanna passed a weary hand across her forehead and hair. "It's hard to know what Margie would think now."

"Don't tell me, after all the trouble we've been through, that you're going to backslide into a sense of duty!" Eve cried.

"There wasn't any miracle — not for long," Joanna went on thoughtfully. "He's just the same. I guess at his age people don't change much."

"Look, Joanna, if you've got some lunatic idea of dedicating the rest of your life to him — "

"Well, you see, now he's lost you too," Joanna explained. "He knows that, by now. He's in the studio with the door shut. I think I know what he's going through in there. Once after Mother left I opened the studio door without knocking — he was on his knees by the sofa with his head in his arms. I tried to back out but he heard the door. He threw a bottle of turpentine at me, and it broke against the door-casing. I've never opened the door since then without knocking."

Eve stood still with a hand braced either side of the open bag, staring down at the contents.

"What shall I do?" she asked, of nobody in particular — unless it was Margie. "You say yourself he can't change now."

"I think you had better just go and ask Richie to drive you to the station." Joanna gave her an indulgent, adult smile, and shook her head so that the pale hair swung. "You don't think I *believe* what you said this afternoon, do you?" she asked gently. "About my pouring the tea because Margie meant me to take her place."

"Why not? It figures."

"Didn't you see Richie's face? You were looking straight at him." Joanna rose and came across the room and kissed Eve's cheek. "It was just like a book," she said. "But I hope he knows I'm not counting on it. Have you got everything? You walk straight down the stairs and out the door with your bag and don't stop for anything."

"Joanna, I'm not going without you. Get a coat and come with me now, tonight. You'll never do it otherwise."

"No, I couldn't. Thank you just the same."

"I will not leave you here like this," Eve said, planting herself. "Especially not in any such Joan of Arc frame of mind. Hurry up, grab a coat and never mind about packing a bag, I'll lend you things."

"I can't." Joanna closed Eve's bag with a double snap, lifted it from the luggage-rack, and handed it to her. "You'd better get away while he's still in the studio, or there'll be another row."

"And leave you to face the music? I will not!"

"He'll be all right with me, once you're out of the house."

"Sometimes I even wonder if you're safe here."

"Oh, nonsense." Joanna could smile tolerantly at that. "He doesn't drink, and he's never thrown anything but once. I'd worry about him all night if I left like that."

"And *I'll* have a sleepless night if you stay here! Please get your coat, like a sensible girl."

"Eve, he'll need somebody. He'll be an absolute angel to me for a while. I'm not afraid of him at times like this. In fact, I'm not ever afraid of *him* — I'm only afraid of scenes. At his very worst he'd never — *hurt* me."

"You mean he wouldn't beat you up, or go for you with a carving-knife."

"No, of course he wouldn't!" smiled Joanna.

For a moment Eve juggled the idea of telling her what no one else knew — that there was no blood relationship between herself and the man she called father. It was,

Eve felt, a very dangerous knowledge. Possessing it, she held the whip-hand over Beau Marshall — an advantage which he had surrendered to her voluntarily because he had fallen in love with her. To use it against him would be a betrayal of his confidence, given at a rare moment of genuine emotion on his part — Eve had always believed that words spoken in love had anyway the sanctity of the confessional.

But not only that. It was a knowledge which would bring down Joanna's world as well, and could only come as a profound shock to her at the very least, raising questions which must drastically affect her future from that moment. Unaware, Joanna still had a pattern of daily life to which she was accustomed, within which she existed with some basic security. Once she knew, a fundamental change was entailed. Eve drew back from so monstrous an act of further interference. She must find some other way. . . .

"You come with me tonight or I don't go myself," she said firmly. "Later, if you're sure you want to come back — very well, we'll go into it then." She set down the bag. "I'm going to wait right here on the burning deck till you get that coat."

"Well — I'll go as far as Richie's with you — "

"Good. He'll see to the rest of it."

Joanna opened the door cautiously and listened, then fled across the passage to her room, returning only seconds later wearing a grey tweed coat, hatless, but carrying a handbag which held her key and a little money. Eve picked up her luggage, and together they tiptoed down the upper hall and the stairs.

As they reached the bottom step the studio door opened and Marshall stood there. They paused instinctively, staring back at him in guilty silence.

"Wholesale treachery and desertion, I see," he remarked, motionless in his doorway. His smooth face looked white and drawn, but he carried himself with his usual tailored erectness and habitual lack of superfluous, lounging movement.

"I'm sorry, Beau — but I've got to go back to New York tonight and I'm taking Joanna with me."

"Shall I call a cab?" he asked courteously, and his face was rigid.

"We're going to ask Richie to drive us to the station," Eve said unwillingly, for that was really rubbing it in.

"Which he will do with pleasure, I'm sure."

When Eve moved forward Joanna stood still, her eyes on his face. Eve reached back and caught her by the arm and Joanna followed her slowly, blindly, looking back.

"Not even good-bye and so long?" he asked quietly, as the knob turned under Eve's hand.

"Good-bye, Beau," she said gently, and Joanna broke

away from her without a sound and ran to him and laid her arms around his shoulders.

"It's all right, Father — I'm not going," she whispered, and hid her face against him.

Motionless in her embrace, explicitly doing nothing to hold her there, he smiled bleakly at Eve over Joanna's head.

"Please observe," he said, "that I have not forced her to this decision."

"*You have no right to her!*" she cried, and their eyes locked and held, with the secret between them. She had the means and the power to wreck him, to turn his whole life against him, like a knife-blade. A few hasty words from her to Joanna now, and nothing would ever be the same again. His so vulnerable pride was at her mercy, his façade, the fabric of his daily existence, the only claim he had on human companionship and affection, could be damaged beyond repair if she chose.

He saw that she held the weapon in her hands, hesitating to use it, but he made no threat and no appeal. He simply waited, with Joanna's arms around him, with nothing on his face even to remind Eve of how she had come by the knowledge which was to have died with him — till his need of her had grown greater than his need of the illusion.

"I told you I couldn't do it," Joanna was saying, muffled, her face hidden.

"You may change your mind about that," Eve said. "If you do, you know where to come."

And she went, closing the door behind her. Coward . . . but there must be some other way . . .

In the hall by the studio door, Marshall laid his arms around the slender body which clung to him protectively.

"Thank you, Totsy," he said, and drew a long, cautious breath as though testing release from intolerable pain. "We'll get along, won't we. There's still two of us — isn't there."

"And we're both in the same boat." She drew away from him and dropped the coat from her shoulders on to a chair. "Eve got her wires crossed this afternoon. You realize, don't you, darling, that it's not me that's going to take Margie's place."

"Eve — *and Richie?*"

She saw him put out a hand, groping for the door-casing, and he leaned against it heavily. She went to him and took his other arm.

"Come and sit down. I'll make you a drink. Don't take it too hard, Father. Eve only came here for the week-end, she said so herself — she never really belonged to us." She guided him to the sofa in the studio and pushed him down on to it. "You sit there, I'll fix you up." She went to the tray on a table against the wall, and splashed whiskey into a glass and carried it to him, neat.

"You drink that, and sit tight. I'll do a better one later, with ice and soda."

He sat with the glass in his hand.

"Are you sure about — them?" he asked.

"Quite sure, Father. Richie's poor face when she tossed me at him this afternoon!"

"But — they hardly know each other!"

"They've met in town. She told me. And it doesn't have to take long, does it."

"How she must have laughed at me," he said.

"No, she never did that, I know." Joanna came and sat down beside him and linked her arm through his. "In fact, she's not even sure about Richie herself yet — wasn't, when she left here. But she'll find out now. We've lost them, darling — or rather, we never had them to lose."

The glass slid from his hand to the floor, spilling the whiskey in a widening pool on the rug. He twisted suddenly and hid his face in her lap, and Joanna sat holding him, pouring over him the warmth of her youth and pity and loyalty, because Richie almost without lifting a finger had done it again.

xvi

IT was nearly dark in the street, and Richie's lights were on. A car was parked in the drive below the steps. The house looked warm and bright and comforting as Eve turned in on the gravel, carrying her bag, almost at a run, and flung herself at the bell. While she waited for the door to open she tried by will power to slow the beating of her heart, and failed.

Richie opened the door himself, a cigarette in his other hand. Behind him in the living-room the radio news was on, and she could see Stella and Jerome sitting on the sofa with cocktails in their hands.

Richie was startled to see her, reached for her with a welcoming gesture, took the bag from her, and closed the door almost as though she might be pursued.

"What happened? I've been worried — " Even now his voice was unhurried and gentle.

"I tried to bring Joanna away with me. She wouldn't

come," Eve said faintly with a note of apology. "I want to catch the train. She said you'd take me to the station."

"Yes, of course. But there isn't a train till — "

"Nine-thirty, I know!" she interrupted hysterically. "But I want to go now! I'll wait there."

"You'd better come along in and have a drink and some dinner first. Plenty of time — "

"Thank you very much, but I — " She glanced past him into the living-room — Margie's room — one of the things she had to get away from. "I know I shouldn't ask you to leave now, but if it isn't too inconvenient will you please take me to the station?"

He looked down at her a moment, puzzled but sympathetic, picked up the bag again, and opened the door for her.

"We'll take Jerome's car," he said, going to where it stood below the steps. "He won't mind." He helped her into it, put her bag in the back, and slid under the wheel. Lights came on at his touch, the engine answered the starter, gravel crunched under the tires.

Eve sat beside him, wilted and speechless, her hands lying loose in her lap. Once she stole a look at his face in the upward light from the dashboard. She remembered how he had one day taken Joanna into his car, giving her a chance to regain composure. Everybody ran to Richie. He was that kind of guy.

The silence lengthened.

Richie was up a tree and out on a limb. He had wakened this morning convinced that he would always love and cherish Joanna as a sort of living legacy of happy association from his life with Margie. But Joanna was a decorative slate with very little written on it. Joanna, he finally faced it, was so far as he was concerned hopelessly young. He found himself quite appalled by the idea of undertaking from the beginning the education of anyone so vulnerable and pitiful and — ignorant as Joanna. Richie wanted to be met halfway. And Eve, with her lowered eyelids, veiling knowledge, her discreet lips, already shaped to love, her impulsive hands, schooled to quietness — Eve had still come towards him.

When Eve arrived at his house for tea that afternoon it was all he could do, and his own self-discipline was boundless, not to allow his mounting excitement and certainty to show. It wouldn't have mattered with Jerome and Stella, but the presence of the Marshalls was sufficient to put him on his guard. At the same time, if he had been ticking over as he should have been, he might have had the wits to foresee the disastrous result of putting Joanna in Margie's chair at the tea-table. But he was unaccustomed to being on his guard, with Margie it had never been necessary. He had had some dim idea of showing Joanna that she would always have a place in his home, that not even his feeling for Eve would ever eliminate her old privileges there. And so, shielding Joanna from his own guilt over a situation which did not yet exist except in his own mind, he had unwittingly caused the roof to fall in.

Eve, misreading his action and trying to help, had made that misbegotten little speech which turned his kindhearted gesture towards Joanna into a declaration of intentions he did not possess. It had hushed Beau Marshall, which was what she aimed to do, and given him something to think about. It was just the sort of eerie idea to appeal to Beau. It did not at all appeal to Richie, who knew that Margie was not like that. Margie was a great let-be-er. He could not imagine that she would reach back from the grave to impose a pattern of her own devising on people who still had lives to live. Margie was gone, Richie believed, into some dwelling-place of light and peace — which she had earned. He did not want to believe that she was still encumbered with earthly dilemmas and uncertainties. Wherever Margie was now, the answers were known. Those who were left behind must work out their own answers.

This he had done to his own satisfaction, and he was still shaken by the implications of Eve's foolhardy attempt to work the oracle for him. She had perhaps raised hopes in Joanna which were already doomed, and Beau would be expecting results which, however unwelcome to him, could cause awkwardness and confusion when they failed to materialize. Even Jerome and Stella had now been put on the wrong track.

Richie had found it impossible to communicate to them anything of his own preoccupation, and was thankful for the small routine it required to prepare drinks and turn on the news, to cover the time following the departure of his guests. Even so, he felt their acute awareness of a mood which they of course must be attributing to the wrong source. The scene Beau had made was of less importance than its aftermath — and idiotic, wrongheaded Eve, having mistaken all the signs and guessed all the wrong answers, had landed everybody in a hell of a misunderstanding.

Nothing fatal, of course, Richie was reflecting with his usual unstampedable tolerance of life's recurrent crises, as he drove. Poor Joanna had long since learned to expect very little. To Joanna he was merely King Arthur and the Samaritan and maybe God's kid brother, but Joanna's prince was still to come. It might be something of a trick to get her to see that now, but it would be up to him to handle it. Eve had at least succeeded in establishing communications, and the thing now was to keep the line open between Joanna and the outside world. He thought of Marshall and winced. That was a tough one. Eve hadn't known her own strength. He was infinitely relieved that she had come away from the house tonight. There was never any question of physical violence to Joanna — that was not the way Marshall worked. But this new factor of his infatuation with Eve was something else again. She must have got some sort of fright, to leave in such a hurry.

Eve felt him glance at her, and refused to meet his eyes, pretending to watch the car ahead. He turned off the main road and into the entrance of an unpaved lane and stopped the car within sight of the passing traffic and switched off the engine, leaving the lights on. Still she could not speak. He took out a packet of cigarettes and held it out to her, and she accepted one, and a light, and he lit his own. Her fingers trembled noticeably, and she knew that he had seen.

"You can't go like this," he said, making it a simple statement of fact. "I've got to know what happened over there."

"I left her with him," Eve said. "That's what happened."

"Was there a row?"

"No. Not exactly. It was Joanna's choice. Oh, Richie, I feel such a fool!"

"I know," he said, and sighed. "I know all about that. Well — you tried." He pulled out the ashtray in the dashboard and settled back, hatless, composed, normal, as though they had all night. "Come on, now, from the beginning. What gave you the shakes like this?"

"When we got back to the house he asked if I wanted a drink," she began, as bidden. "I said No thanks, and went straight up to my room. I don't know how to tell you what I — what I thought while I sat there, it — I — well, I suddenly got a sort of panic and began to pack."

"Don't skip," he admonished kindly, and she sat silent a moment as though reconstructing the thing in her mind. You couldn't tell the man that his wife was acting like a ghost. You couldn't possibly put it into words to Richie that you had seemed to feel the pressure of an intangible hand, hustling you in a direction you didn't want to go, or account for that involuntary leap of nerves when the glass vase crashed on the dressing-table — too late she remembered the drip of water on to the carpet. Neither she nor Joanna had done anything about that. . . .

"Joanna came to my room just about the time that I realized I must see her before I left the house," she stumbled on, because he was waiting. "She said an extraordinary thing — she came to make sure that I was going to get away." Eve glanced at him again and saw that he was not surprised. "She said that for a while she had wanted me to stay there and look after Beau — but then she realized she didn't want me to get caught up in it the way she was." He nodded silently, as though he had expected something of the kind, and Eve hurried her story ahead towards the point where he would have to comment, at its end. "I tried to persuade her to come away with me tonight. Finally I refused to go without her. Then she got a coat and we went downstairs. He heard us, I suppose. Anyway, he appeared from the studio before we got out the door. He — didn't argue. He just stood there, looking ghastly. There was nothing about him to — to hit against. She went to him. She stayed with him. I just — couldn't seem to do anything about it." Eve put her face in her hands, and he made no move to comfort her, sitting relaxed and thoughtful, his own hands resting on the wheel.

"Poor Eve," he said at last, and "*Poor Joanna!*" she cried rebelliously behind her hands.

"Joanna's grown up, all of a sudden," he said, sitting quietly behind the wheel. "Hadn't you noticed?"

"Oh, Richie, you will get her out of there now, and see that she has some kind of life?"

"You've put me on kind of a spot with Joanna, you realize that, don't you."

"She's in love with you, Richie. She always has been."

"There you have it," he said. "She always has been — because I am about the only man she has ever had a chance to think about. Margie and I were a shining example of what every girl naturally wants, so Joanna naturally thinks it's me she wants. If she gets out and about a little more, she'll soon learn that there are other men — younger ones, incidentally. Joanna and I are used to each other — I look safe to her, and she's pretty well an open book to me. We might get along all right on that, lots of people do, but the chances are that she'd outgrow it if I didn't. Anyway, it doesn't set any worlds on fire." His eyes rested on Eve's face in the dim light — humorous, patient, very knowing. "Does it," he added, and waited.

"Do you — think things should just go up in smoke?" she inquired, feeling unaccountably shy, with a singing in her ears.

"They can," he said, doing nothing whatever about it.

"I guess I've done everything all wrong," she reflected, sounding young and dismal. "But it did seem as though I got some kind of message this afternoon — to say what I did. I hope you don't mind my bringing Margie into it like that, but I did honestly feel — "

Something in his quiet look stopped her, though he did not interrupt. *Didn't you see Richie's face? You were looking straight at him*, Joanna had said. Yes, she had seen Richie's face. She saw it now, in the pale glow from the dashboard, tender and alight with a kind of compassionate amusement — but silent, as was his exasperating way. . . .

"P-please don't laugh at me," she murmured foolishly.

"Who's laughing?"

But she knew that the corners of his mouth were tucked in. Perhaps if he knew the rest of it — the part that wasn't hers to tell — the part that, whatever one believed about Beau Marshall, still left a nagging doubt about Joanna's remaining in his house — it might not be cricket, but what was a man like Richie for, if one had to keep secrets from him?

"There's something more," she said slowly. "I didn't mean to tell you, but it's heavy on my mind. It makes such a difference." Characteristically he put no question into her pause, he merely smoked and waited, and so, having started, she had to go on. "Richie, she's not Beau's child. There's no blood tie between them. He told me himself this morning. You were all wrong about his wife, apparently. She was no good — ever. It went on for years, and out of pride he covered up for her, even to raising Joanna as his own."

"Is *that* what it is!" he murmured, and —

"Aren't you ever surprised at *anything?*" she cried.

"I'm very surprised. I knew there must be something — but I never thought of that."

"I nearly told her tonight — but I thought I had persuaded her to come away without that. Then I nearly charged him with it in front of her. But somehow I couldn't bring myself to, there were so many — imponderables — "

"No," he murmured, staring out through the windshield. "No, you were right not to. The poor b — son-of-a-gun hardly deserved that, no matter what."

"Why do we always let him off!" she said crossly.

"But I go on wondering — was I wrong to leave her there, now that I know?"

His eyes came round to her gravely.

"It's not really any different between them than before he told you," he pointed out.

"That's what I was counting on, but — you do think she's all right there — alone — ?"

"Why, sure." His tone carried real conviction, which concurred with her own.

"But not — forever," she qualified, with a nod to the conventions at least.

"No. Certainly not forever, I agree."

He pressed the starter and backed the car and drove out on to the main road again. Eve sat silent, puzzled, a little disappointed. He had made it fairly plain that he had no intention of marrying Joanna after all. And it was fairly plain that she herself was the reason, if she had read his silences right — as even Joanna had seemed to imply. And then — nothing. They were on the way to the station, the dim privacy of the lane left behind. She must have made another mistake. Perhaps in her preoccupation over Joanna, she had seemed coy or hard to get, or had missed some cue. . . . This, she told herself, was intolerable, this schoolgirl tumult of uncertainty and impatience and sky-rocketing excitement. No man could do this to her. Not any more.

"I haven't forgotten anything," he spoke softly against

the whir of the engine. "But I have no intention of making love to you in a parked car." The road was straight and empty before him, and he dropped one hand on hers in her lap briefly, and glanced down at her with a rueful, appreciative smile. "You'll have to wait," he said. "I'll ring you up on Monday."

"The telephone's not much good either," she remarked, and he laughed out loud — which she thought she had never heard before.

"The telephone is a means to an end," he said, as they drove into the lighted station yard.

xvii

BUT the first time the telephone rang on Monday it was Tad. The office had all read the new script, and there was much enthusiasm, and he wanted to talk. How about lunch?

With the events of the past week-end weighing down her conscience, she agreed to lunch. There were quite a few things to break to Tad, and it was a question how much — or how little — she was going to tell him. He hadn't even known she was going to Beau Marshall's for a weekend. . . .

She sat with her elbows on the desk and her head in her hands. *I can't.* It's all a bad dream. It never happened. I've been sitting right here ever since Friday. I'll forget the whole thing. I'll start a new book. I'll tell Richie —

The telephone rang again, and she snatched it with cold, damp fingers.

"Good morning," said Richie in his understated way. "Just as I thought, I'm in a jam down here. Got to go to Washington. Upsets all our plans."

"We didn't have any plans," she objected faintly.

"Didn't we?"

She hesitated too long.

"Well, anyway," he continued unruffled, "I can't get out of this till about Thursday, from the looks of it. I'll have to leave it like that, and call you again. Think you can stay out of trouble for a few days?"

"I've got trouble for lunch," she admitted. "In the form of Tad."

"Mm-hm," he agreed. "Watch it now."

"He isn't going to like anything I say. He doesn't even know I went to Beau's last Friday. Oh, Richie, if only I *hadn't!*"

" 'Backward, turn backward, O Time in your flight,' " Richie recited.

"Back of Joanna's first letter, I guess."

"As bad as that?"

"I don't know." She laid the cool mouthpiece of the phone against her forehead. "Richie, I don't know."

"Here, now," he said. "If I wasn't already on one foot for the airport — "

"No, don't come now, I — "

"If I could, you couldn't stop me. What's the matter, Eve? Would you like it in writing?"

She knew how he looked as he said it — amused, compassionate, knowing.

"Oh, *no,* Richie, I just — don't know where I am, I've got a horrible feeling it all happened to two other fellows — "

"Relax, now. We'll live till Thursday, with any luck."

"Richie."

"Hullo?"

"There's nothing wrong, is there? I mean, this Washington trip — ?"

"You mean have they caught up with me at last?" His grin was almost audible. "No — just routine. No bail required. Take it easy, won't you."

"Good-bye — "

"So long." His receiver clicked. He was on the way to the airport.

Eve sat a moment, staring at the telephone. Routine to Washington. For the first time since their first meeting she had time to wonder — what did Richie *do?* I just sit behind a desk in Wall Street, he had said then. Money, or he couldn't live the way he did. Tad would know. Tad knew everything. Except about her week-end. Well, he'd soon be abreast of that too. . . .

Thoughtfully she changed her dress and did her face and chose a hat. Tad liked silly hats. Thoughtfully she arrived on time at their favorite restaurant and their favorite corner table, and Tad ordered her favorite cocktail without having to ask. By the time the waiter returned, Tad had of course noticed something.

"O.K.," he said, lifting his glass to hers. "Tell father what's bothering you. But you are *not* going to get it back to rewrite. You'll spoil it. As a matter of fact, it's gone. Printer's got it."

"Yes," she said, not registering. "Tad, I had a funny sort of week-end."

"I can see that," said Tad. "You died laughing. Where?" he asked, like a doctor — where does it hurt?

"At Beau Marshall's."

It caught Tad with the glass at his lips. He tipped it till it drained down his throat and signalled the waiter for another.

"You might have told me," he said.

"I should have. You might have stopped me."

"Well, drink up, and you'll feel better." He watched her anxiously. "Come on, give," he said, and she shook her head helplessly and tipped her own glass.

"I'd like to get stinking, just this once," she confided.

"Waiter!" said Tad, in some excitement, and she laughed, and at once was serious again. "The trouble is, I seem to have done nothing but tell somebody what somebody else said. Richie made me go into total recall on the way to the station Saturday night, and now I've got to begin all over again for you."

"Was he there too?"

"He lives next door, remember? What does he do, by the way?"

"For a living? Wall Street. He was something very hush-hush during the war—had a couple of narrow squeaks, I guess."

"Is it hush-hush when he goes to Washington?"

"Does he?"

"He's there now."

"That's good. What did *he* do on this famous week-end?"

"He came to dinner. I don't know where to start," she confessed miserably, baffled again by the necessity to tell Tad after all these comfortable years that in a few days she had allowed Richie Forrest to take possession of her life.

"Week-ends usually start on Friday," he suggested. "How did you get to Beau Marshall's?"

"He drove me up. They both wrote and invited me. He hung it on that illustrating job. He had a layout to show me. In case."

"Fast worker, eh?"

"It was a good layout," she said. "I'd like to use it." Her lips curled in intentional, clowning self-consciousness. "It looked like me, only younger. Very subtle."

"Very. So what then? What's the daughter like, by the way?"

"Oh, Joanna is adorable."

"*What?*"

"She is, Tad. Beautiful in a fragile, pathetic way — and brave, too." Eve sighed. "It's an *endless* story. And now that I'm back home, with everything just as I left it, I can't believe any of it happened! I said to Richie this morning, I feel as though it must have been two other fellows."

"This morning?" Tad stiffened like a bird-dog.

"On the phone."

"I see." He picked up the menu and glanced at the hovering waiter. "I'm going to need some food. Something sustaining. Roast beef?"

"Yes, please. Anything."

When the waiter had gone —

"And how about Marshall?" Tad resumed. "Was he adorable too?"

"You can't help feeling sorry for him, Tad."

"I bet *I* could. Did you try?"

"I had to try. Very hard."

"You are overdoing the suspense element in this yarn," Tad said judiciously. "Your point of attack is too long delayed. You should study the works of a gal named Eve Endicott, who is famous for always establishing her story line if not also reader-identification within the first ten pages."

Eve laughed, with a little appealing gesture of both hands.

"It's not my story! I said to Joanna I was thankful I didn't have to write it! And she said I *was* writing it." Eve sobered. "But I wasn't. Margie wrote it."

"Margie," said Tad, ominously calm. "Never heard of her."

"She was Richie's wife. She's dead."

"But she wrote this week-end," said Tad, remaining sane by an outstanding effort.

"You see? You don't believe it!"

"I haven't got anything yet to believe!" he cried, and his voice cracked a little. "What's the matter with you? Did you fall in love with Marshall, or what?"

"He fell in love with me," she said quietly, looking down.

"Oh-oh. I might have known."

She found it impossible then to add, But I fell in love with Richie Forrest. She sat staring down at the table in front of her, appalled all over again by the colossal task of fitting the past week-end into the rest of her life. Fortunately at that point the food arrived and the waiter fussed around. Tad was one of those men who have an effect on waiters. They mothered him. When he finally got rid of this one, he turned a still dazed but expectant face towards Eve.

"And now," he intoned nasally, "after a brief message from our sponsor we will return to the second act of our story, which is entitled *Eve Throws a Monkey-wrench into the Works.*"

"Oh, Tad, I haven't even begun to tell you!"

Tad had a reluctant and soundless but explosive laugh, the remnants of a schoolboy's spluttering snicker, which then creased his long face into lines of humorous aftermath.

"You're doin' all right," he said when he could. "How far does this take us? To Friday night?"

"Saturday morning."

He waved an admonishing finger.

"Tell about Friday night first," he insisted.

"That was when Richie came to dinner, along with some other people. Joanna did a nice little job as hostess, I was proud of her. Everything was perfectly charming — including Beau Marshall. Till I began to think What's all the fuss about? The man's as normal as blueberry pie."

"Mm-hm?" Tad began on his roast beef.

"But the next morning we went into the studio to see the thing he had dreamed up for the illustration — "

"Which was good."

"Which was very good, and I said so. And the next thing I knew — "

"He made a pass at you. That figures."

"*I'm* telling this," Eve reminded him. "Then it all came out about Margie, who has become a local legend. You see, both Joanna and Beau had a Thing about my being like her. Everybody out there has a Thing about Margie, who was completely devoted to Richie and he to her. But Beau had been in love with her for years in a mad, monastic sort of way — apparently she knew how to manage him, so far as anybody could. And since she died he's had no — no balance-wheel."

Tad shook his head ruefully above his plate.

"It'll never sell," he said.

"No, it wouldn't, I quite agree, I know how impossible it sounds! You have to live in that house with the Marshalls to understand how it is haunted, and I don't use the word loosely, by a woman whom everyone worshipped and who seems even now to — to influence their lives. You see, Tad — I felt her too. It was Margie, not Beau Marshall, that I ran away from."

She had him now.

"Evie, for cryin' out loud — !"

"Yes, I know, it's Monday morning. But I was there at twilight on Saturday." She pushed the food around on her plate, not looking at him. "So was Margie," she said.

"What was she trying to do to you?"

"It seems she had promised me to Beau Marshall — if he was a good boy and always ate his spinach." Eve swallowed. "I don't think Margie had counted on my falling in love with Richie."

Tad's knife dropped on to the plate with an audible

thud. He kept his head down. Then after a long moment his shoulders began to shake, and he gave his modified schoolboy splutter of mirth.

"I know it isn't funny," he said, when he could. "Especially for me. But I suddenly thought of Joanna. You go tearing off on this almighty crusade to rescue Joanna, and you came back two days later having annexed *both* her men!" And he sat amid the ruins and wept with laughter.

"Well, it's not quite as simple as that," Eve said with some dignity, as soon as she could make him hear.

"I'm sure it isn't," he agreed, and took off his spectacles and wiped his eyes with his napkin. "It's like being shot," he explained. "I don't feel anything yet. When's the wedding?"

"I said it wasn't simple."

"Margie seems to me to have had more sense than anybody," he remarked. "She got out and stayed out. At least — " He was threatened again with hysterics and overcame it. "How did she — I mean, how did you know — I mean, did you *see* anything?"

"Something draped in a sheet that vanished?" Eve suggested with a weary smile. "No. She was more subtle than that. It's all in their minds, I said to myself — and then I felt my own mind going the same way. I can't expect you, stuffing yourself with roast beef the way you are, to believe me when I say that Margie tried to deliver me as a living sacrifice to Beau Marshall — and then tried, through me, to hand Joanna over to Richie. But *I* believe in Margie — even at this distance. It's partly thanks to Joanna that Margie didn't get her way. Joanna has grown up — all of a sudden."

"Yes, it's still Joanna's story, isn't it," Tad said more seriously. "As of now, what are Joanna's prospects?"

"She's still there, in the house with Beau, because she herself chose to stay there. I don't approve, and we've got to get her out. But it will be easier now."

"And what will Margie say to that?"

"I think Margie will have to be — exorcised. If one can exorcise a saint. Once I almost thought I saw my way to it. You can see how out of focus I got — I almost contemplated taking over Margie's job." Eve shook her head. "Maybe I'm wrong, at that. Maybe even now we don't know what Margie really wants. It's hard to tell what a ghost wants. You feel them crowding you — urging you — you feel there *is* something you must do, to satisfy them — but the veil is too heavy between — they can't get through — or you are too stupid. Margie was there in Beau's house. She was trying to tell me something. Why else was I there? She loved them all so much — but she couldn't do it alone, even when she was alive. I bungled it somehow. I wasn't psychic enough. Whatever it was, I did it all wrong. I wonder if she'll go on trying."

"You really got yourself into this thing, didn't you," Tad said, watching her. "You really burnt your fingers."

"I'm still in it. Coming back to New York hasn't let me off. I had to leave Joanna there, with Beau. But that isn't the end of it. We've got to get her out — open the doors — see that she makes friends in spite of Beau — "

"And eventually marry her off to somebody," Tad suggested intelligently. "Richie, I gather, won't play that game."

"He says he's too old."

"I can imagine how he feels. Now, I've got that nice, Harvard-size nephew who isn't doing anything much. Shall I shine him up and send him round?"

"By all means. But it never works when you want it to," she reflected gloomily. "It has to be an accident, apparently. Tad, I've been wondering — would Frances help?"

"Match-make? She'd love to!"

"How far are you from where Beau and Richie live?"

"About twenty minutes by car."

"If I came to your place for the week-end and Frances asked them to lunch — you and I could just drive over and invite them, so Beau couldn't refuse — "

"Why include him?"

"We've got to break this thing down," she said impatiently. "Let daylight into it — knock off the cobwebs. Once Joanna and Frances are acquainted and she meets some of your friends in a normal sort of way, everybody's going to like her — she's pretty, and she knows how to behave — then Frances could see that she got asked other places, with or without Beau."

"But I thought he would never allow her to fraternize."

"He will now," Eve said significantly.

"You mean, he's reformed?"

"I think I am in a position to see that he does," Eve said darkly.

"You enthrall me. What have you got on him, for God's sake?"

"Enough."

"Evie — !" He gazed at her delightedly.

"No, I can't tell you that part. But *he* knows it's pointed at him like a gun. And if I have to use it as a lever for Joanna's sake I will. He'll put up with just about anything rather than have her find out what I happen to know. Is it all right if I come up to your place next week-end?"

"I'll die if you don't, now!"

"Then on Saturday morning you and I are going to drop in on the Marshalls, all neighborly, and invite them to drive back with us to lunch."

"Wait till I get my bullet-proof vest," said Tad. "What if he just says No-thanks?"

"Then she'll come without him."

"He won't stop her?"

"Not with me standing there, he won't."

"Mightn't it make trouble for her later?"

"He's not the murdering type. Any trouble of his kind, and she comes to me for a nice long visit. Or else."

"Jeepers," said Tad. "Eve Endicott rides again. This I gotta see."

xviii

EVE found it a long week to live through, especially as she hadn't much of anything laid out to do. She was already in that state of stale sag which follows the completion of a script, before the first faint stirrings of the next one are felt. She was temporarily emptied out, emotionally and professionally, and should have spent her time systematically catching up on personal contacts, new plays, and other people's books — filling up the cistern, she called it. But this time she merely wandered around the apartment reading this and that, killing time with television, losing her appetite, and working up a stage-fright about Richie.

She knew she had no sales resistance whatever to Richie. He would come back from Washington and ask her to have lunch or dinner — and with a restaurant table between them propose marriage? Not Richie. But if she asked him to pick her up at the apartment and have a drink there, it amounted to flinging herself into his arms. To achieve any sort of privacy with Richie was difficult. Week-ends were not possible because, unlike Tad, he had no resident propriety in the form of a sister. Richie had something much worse. He had Margie.

This was the nightmare that overhung those dragging days of suspense while she waited for him to come back from Washington. She knew that she could never live there in Margie's house, and she felt no certainty at all that Richie would be willing to uproot, sell out, start all over again, in a house which would be all hers, with no associations, and not next door to Beau Marshall. Richie had said at that first luncheon that the idea of beginning all over again with a stranger was not for him. But Joanna would have fitted into the house without a ripple. Suppose he expected Eve Endicott to do the same.

This was the nightmare. How soon they would come to it. What she was going to say. How he was going to react. Joanna wouldn't have minded Margie. How would it be possible to convey to him that to Eve, Margie was a ghost? It would take all her courage to make him choose between them — because she could lose. Of course it was morbid to suppose that Richie would choose a dead memory over a living woman. But then, when the time came to pack his personal belongings and close the door forever on all the rest — he might still meet regret and resentment, instead of release. How much would the new love be worth to him, compared to what Margie had left behind her? Nobody could live up to what Richie had the right to expect after that.

But you must not compromise, Eve told herself sanely, you must not dodge the issue. He must understand at once that you must start fresh, on your own, with no haunts. It might not come up at once. You can't lunge into it, you have to wait for him to ask. He might take it for granted. If he knew in time he might even draw back. Well, you can't tell him you won't live there till he asks you to! What will he say first? What will I say then? Yes, Richie, yes, *if* I can have my own house. But it won't be like that. He will kiss you, just once, and you'll forget all the ifs and buts and ands. . . .

Thursday morning at last, and the phone ringing.

"Well, I made it. How about dinner tonight?"

"Y-yes, I — "

"Any special place?"

"Well, no, I hadn't thought — "

"I can't dress, I'm just off the plane. Suppose I come round to your place about six-thirty and we'll work it out from there."

"That's fine."

"What's the matter?"

"Nothing's the matter, I just — "

"Remember me? I'm Richie Forrest."

"I *know!*"

"Well, I wasn't sure. You sound sort of absent-minded this morning."

"I was just thinking, we could have a drink here while we decide where to go."

"We could. Six-thirty."

That settled that. If only the rest was as easy.

Richie didn't rush his fences. His handclasp when he entered the apartment lingered a little — his smile was tender, his eyes were amused. Eve's outward composure matched his, and she mixed their martinis with a steady hand, while bells rang inside her like a carillon. When she turned from the tray with a glass in each hand he had roamed gently about the room, finding himself. He accepted the cocktail gravely, and they took the first sip standing. Then he put his free hand on her waist and moved her to the sofa.

"I haven't been able to think of any way to lead up to it," he confessed in his usual muted tone. "Ordinarily it would be much too soon, but things have kind of forced our hand." He set down his glass. "Let's not pretend. You know perfectly well that I want to marry you, just as soon as possible. But there's something on your mind, isn't there. Is it still Joanna?"

"N-no, I — I suppose we'll find some other solution for Joanna."

"I'm afraid we'll have to." He waited. "This reservation in your mind," he said. "Don't you think you could tell me what it is?"

"I suppose I've got to try. This could ruin our evening, Richie. Hadn't we better — "

"I think we had better find out what it is."

Perhaps it would be easier if he couldn't see her face. She rose and turned away from him, carrying the glass, and heard him getting dutifully to his feet behind her.

"It's — Margie," she said, standing at the window with her back to him.

"What about her?" He stayed where he was, beside the sofa.

"I don't know if you realize how it seems to someone who comes in from the outside. But to me — Margie is still there. I was conscious of her the whole time."

"Where?" said Richie, and for the first time in her experience there was an edge to his voice, so that she turned to him confused and questioning.

"Wh-what — ?" she asked stupidly.

"Margie is still where?" said Richie, and in another man the query would have been sharp.

"In Beau's house — I — " She stopped, realizing what she had said.

"Not in mine," said Richie, standing very still, pinning it down.

"N-no — except — well, I wasn't in yours very long, I — " He was waiting for her to finish the incoherence which was all she seemed capable of. "In the lilac room," she added gropingly. "It was always strongest there — as though she *wanted* something of me — as though she had it all figured out for me to marry Beau and you to marry Joanna — " Eve pushed back her hair with a distracted, pathetic gesture. "I didn't mean to — dump it out like this, I — well, I got frightened of Margie, I felt I was crossing her up, when I — when you — Margie had promised me to Beau. He said so."

"*He* said so," Richie repeated, with what was for him emphasis.

"Yes, he — well, it *was* his idea, wasn't it," she conceded in some surprise. "And Joanna's. You think maybe just the power of suggestion — from them — could be strong enough to make me feel — " She looked at him doubtfully, gripping her glass with cold, tense fingers. "She isn't — isn't like that in your house?" she faltered.

"No. I wouldn't do that to her," he said simply.

"I — don't think I — " She was a little uncomprehending.

"So they're still at it," he said, and there seemed to be anger in the words. "I hoped by now it would be over." He moved slowly across the room and took the glass away from her and set it down and held both her cold hands in his warm ones. "You've got it all wrong," he said kindly. "Margie wouldn't wish Beau on to anybody, she knows him too well."

"You don't think — she was trying to tell me — "

"Of course not."

"Then why did I feel — "

"Think back. Beau began it, as though she was on his side, didn't he. Joanna has been well coached, and she doubtless put it to you some other way. And you fell for it. You started pinning things on Margie yourself. All Margie wants is to get away from that relentless grief of theirs. If you felt anything at all, you felt that. They won't let her go."

"Yes, I — do see what you mean," Eve said quietly, and it was as though he had opened something somewhere and let light in. Richie made it so simple, what Margie wanted. Only to rest in peace. Not to be dragged back, and clung on to, and endlessly mourned. That was what Eve had felt in the lilac room — just a striving to be free, like a beating of wings. She herself had known the same sensation of captivity in the smothering possessiveness of Beau's house. Richie was looking down at her, enigmatic, smiling, patient — the way he had looked in the car. She wondered if one was ever able to tell what he was thinking. Joanna said not. But a less haunted man Eve had never seen. "Oh, Richie, I feel a little better," she cried gratefully. "But then why did I say that about Joanna pouring the tea, if there was nothing in it at all — "

"You were just talking off the top of your head," he

said sensibly. "I must say for a moment you made my blood run cold."

Still she doubted that it was quite as simple as he made it sound, and searched his face anxiously. There was nothing there to found such a suspicion on. Very well, those were Richie's terms, no matter what he might think — and if you took Richie you did so on his terms, and lucky at that.

"But you did say," she reminded him obstinately, "that time we had lunch, that it felt right to you with Joanna in the house."

"She made it less empty, yes. I think I was going a little nuts myself, living there alone."

So now they came to it. Now was the time to tell him that unlike Joanna she could never fill that emptiness herself — that she could not stand in for Margie, *would* not, anywhere, for anybody, and that even now, no matter what he said, it was still the house where he and Margie had lived together.

She took her hands from his, and walked away from him down the room.

"There's something else," he said patiently, watching her go. "Let's clean it all up right now, shall we?"

All she had to say was, Richie, I can't live there, don't ask me to live in Margie's house. But the *trouble* that put him to — the upheaval — the expense — the possible regrets . . . Now was the time, in case he wanted to quit.

Now was the time, before things went up in smoke. It's Margie or me, Richie, you've got to choose . . .

"Eve."

She turned distractedly, the room between them.

"Come here," he said almost inaudibly, and when she still hesitated, he jabbed a masterful forefinger towards the floor at his feet. "Come here," he repeated.

She came, unwillingly, apprehensively — spinelessly. He gathered her in and kissed her, with authority. Bells rang, sparks flew, and things went up in smoke.

"That makes *me* feel better," he said. "I began to think *I* was imagining things." He held her cradled and comforted, her face against rough tweed, her nose discovering that sometimes he smoked a pipe. "Now," he said, "tell me the rest of it."

She stirred defensively and found herself unable to move.

"It's — that house," she gasped.

"What house?"

"Yours."

"What about it?"

"I c-couldn't live there — "

His hold slackened enough so that he could see her face.

"Why were you afraid to tell me that?"

"Well, I — you were happy there — and I knew *Joanna* wouldn't have minded — "

"I'm not marrying Joanna — am I?" Compassionately, he laid his face against hers, rocking her in his arms. This moment, this freedom, this relief of unuttered laughter had cost him a sleepless night — moving from room to room, so familiar that he had no need of lights, knowing his way like a blind man, with a touch here and there, more affection than guidance — sitting here, sitting there, thinking, remembering, relinquishing — reaching an inevitable decision — a long farewell, without bitterness. "Poor Eve," he said, rocking her. "I'm way ahead of you. The house is on the market — ever since Monday. But you'd better get busy on another one, or I'll move in here."

xix

TAD'S sister Frances, who dearly loved to matchmake, entered with zeal into Eve's proposed campaign of bringing Joanna out. They spent a pleasant hour after dinner on Friday night scheming, and Fran even appeared at breakfast next morning with a list of possible eligibles, on which her own son's name led all the rest. Tad restrained her with difficulty from combing out Harvard that very week-end, and suggested that they start with a mild family meal today, until Joanna got the hang of things. Was Joanna shy, he wanted to know considerately, and Eve said not really, she had a great deal of self-possession if not rattled by Beau.

"I never embarked on a project like this before," Tad said with some satisfaction. "It makes me feel Jovian and paternal. Who was the guy who went round rescuing girls from the Minotaur?"

"Watch out your armor doesn't squeak," said Eve. "And it wasn't Jove, and he wasn't paternal."

"Details," said Tad, waving them off, and Eve noticed that Fran had turned upon even him a fond and speculative eye.

Eve set out with Tad in his car a little before noon, and they arrived without warning at the Marshalls' door. By good fortune they had news, in the form of an appointment with the editor of *Metropolitan Magazine*, to discuss the illustration of Eve's new script — it seemed worth while maintaining contact with Beau on a professional basis, for the sake of their plans for Joanna.

They rang the bell and Joanna opened the door. She was delighted to see Eve, and she seemed happy and composed as she invited them inside and gave a welcoming hand to Tad.

"Have you come to lunch?" she asked hopefully. "Father's in the studio, I'll go and knock."

"Wait," said Eve, and led the way to the drawing-room. "How are things?" she asked quietly when they reached it.

"Surprisingly peaceful so far. He's working very long hours — some new project, I guess, but I don't know what it is, he hasn't asked me to sit nor showed me anything. He's — gone into himself, the way he does."

"Are you all right?" Eve asked.

"Perfectly all right. I told you how it would be. He needs me here."

"We thought it would be nice if you both came back to lunch with us," said Tad, excessively normal.

"Well, it would be very nice — I'll ask him." Joanna turned upon Tad her customary look of childlike, unself-conscious interest.

"He's got the illustrating job with the magazine if he wants it," Eve said, and "Oh, thank you!" Joanna said sincerely to Tad, who hastily disclaimed her gratitude.

"Nothing to do with me, I'm sorry to say — I'm just the book man. Eve fixed it up with Keating, herself. As a matter of fact, I live just across lots from here, you know — we're neighbors. Ought to get acquainted, don't you think?"

"Yes, you two go ahead and do just that," Eve told them approvingly. "I'll go along to the studio and rout him out for lunch."

She approached the studio door with a resolute step and a slight flutter in her midriff. Tad's presence in the drawing-room behind her made a big difference, as she knocked and heard no reply from within. She knocked again and set the door slightly ajar and spoke through the crack.

"Beau, it's Eve. May I come in?"

When there was still no answer she pushed the door open and paused on the threshold. Beau had turned towards her and stood defensively with his back to the easel where he had been working. He wore a faded blue smock and held an oil palette and brushes, and he seemed more incredulous at sight of her than surprised.

"Hi, there," Eve said casually and sauntered in. "Guess what. The magazine came through. Do you still want to sell that layout?"

He laid down everything and wiped his hands on a cloth and threw it aside. Then he came forward, his right hand held out in formal greeting.

"Fairy godmother," he remarked. "Well, why not? It's a role that suits you."

"No hard feelings?" She gave him her hand.

"I suppose gratitude is more in order. It must be a great satisfaction to you — to bring me news like that, and me so undeserving and outcast."

"I'm at Tad's again for the week-end, so he ran me over. He's talking to Joanna in the drawing-room. We thought you might both come back with us to lunch."

"Very thoughtful of you. But I'm working much too hard to go gallivanting."

She threw an involuntary glance at the easel — and then looked again. He was painting a portrait in oils. It looked as though he had done quite a lot of work on it, but it was quite without his usual precision and style. The background was a rather muddy blue, against which he had set a woman's head, turned towards you over her shoulder — the hair was red, and the face was blurred and unfinished except for the grey-green eyes which met yours from the canvas in a wide, following stare. Even if she had never seen the photograph on Richie's piano, Eve would have known that Beau was painting a portrait, from memory, of Margie Forrest.

"Don't look, it's not finished," he said. "She's beginning to come alive, but I haven't quite caught it yet. I can't take anything else on till I do."

"But Beau, what about the illustration?"

"Oh, that. It's ready. Do you want to take it with you?"

"But you'll have to see Keating, and — "

"Sorry, I can't take the time to go up to town now, I've got to get on with this."

"But the other thing is a *job*," she insisted. "You oughtn't to shut yourself up with this, it's — it's not — "

"Not for sale," he suggested. "A waste of time, you feel." He waited, watching her, ironical and defensive.

"Come to lunch, Beau. Do you good."

"No doubt. But not today, thanks."

"We'll take Joanna, then."

"No. I'd rather she didn't go."

Eve sighed, and leaned her elbows on the table, facing him.

"This is it, Beau. Don't make me do it."

"I don't follow." He was wary and smiling.

"Yes, you do."

Their eyes held. It took him a moment to comprehend. When he did, he stood surveying her with his characteristic immobility, and she saw that it was touch and go between his feeling for her, which was still there, and the cold, unapproachable fury which was his habit when cornered.

"You are dictating terms," he said.

"I am in a position to. Most unfairly, I agree. Don't crowd me, Beau. Give me credit, I'd rather not do it this way."

"Oh, all right, lay it on the line. You may as well."

"What's it going to be worth to you — to keep Joanna for your daughter a little while longer, till she marries — which she will. Because I'll make a deal with you — so that the facts do die with you and me."

"You've got me over a barrel, haven't you. How you must be enjoying yourself."

"You're wrong. I hate it. I've never turned a man's confidence against him before. I hope I never do again. But if you don't play ball with me, Beau, you haven't got a daughter, and the whole humiliating story is going to come out. That's not good for Joanna either — but it's better than what she's had so far."

"You've got a price, I suppose."

"Lunch at Tad's today, to start with."

"And then?"

"No more iron curtain. Joanna lives a normal, come-and-go life — friends of her own — a chance to fall in love — a chance to marry. Tad's sister will launch her. She'll make her own way after that."

"So you've brought them in on her side." His eyes flickered.

"Cross my heart, Beau, I haven't told them."

"I suppose you call this letting me off easy."

"I think it's fair enough."

"Why, you gold-plated little blackmailer, you can't do this to me! Nobody can! Take your illustrating job and get out of here! Tell Joanna what you damn' well please — you're bound to, sooner or later!"

"Think it over, Beau. When I do that she will have to leave here. I will ask her to come and stay with me — or she can go to Frances, no doubt, if she prefers."

"She might choose to stay here. She did before."

"She's not a child, Beau."

"You mean it wouldn't be proper. I suppose it isn't anyway."

"It's as proper now as it ever was — so long as she doesn't know. When she does, it becomes — embarrassing."

"At least you trust me to some extent," he said, with irony.

"I've no reason not to. And it would be pretty hard on her, wouldn't it, if I had to bring it up now."

"All right, take her and get out," he said sharply. "I won't interfere with that."

"That's not enough, Beau."

"Eve, will you for God's sake *go*, and leave me alone?"

"Joanna has a very tender heart," she continued, without moving. "And you are all she has ever had to love. She wouldn't go with me on Saturday because she couldn't bear to leave a lonely, embittered, disappointed man she called father. You've done so much for her that was right and good — you could so easily come out way ahead, even now, if you're willing to try. But so long as you mope about this studio, alone, hating me, and generally breaking your poor heart again, all the king's horses and all the king's men can't give Joanna a good time."

"I don't hate you. I wish I did." His voice broke. He sat down with his head in his hands and she stood watching him, her elbows on the table. "Well, what are you waiting for? Call your shots, Eve."

"It's not too hard. And it might get easier as you go on. You get the full treatment too, Beau. It should have happened to you long ago. You come to lunch today, for instance — and no wise-cracks. Pretty soon there'll be a dinner-party — yet get into your little black tie and your dinner jacket and you take Joanna to it, in a new dress. And you *like* it, Beau, because I'll be there watching, and if you backslide and I say Behave yourself, you'd better make an effort. I'll be right behind you all the way, my dear, and I'll help you all I can, but I won't stand any nonsense, you hear?" She bent towards him, smiling, coaxing, imperative. "Come on, Beau, you can do it!"

"Give me a week or two," he temporized. "I must get on with this, while I still remember exactly how she looked. Since you came I — I don't see her so clearly any more."

"Beau, you mustn't go on like this. You asked me one day to save you, and I'm going to, one way or another. Take off that picturesque blue rag and put on your nice tweedy jacket and come along with us." She picked up his jacket off a chair and held it out for him. " 'Tisn't as though I didn't know what you can do when you try."

"Never should have tried," he said with a grimace, but he accepted the jacket in a hypnotized sort of way and shrugged it into place.

"That's my boy!" said Eve heartily, and hit him affectionately on the shoulder and marched him towards the drawing-room.

They were met by a burst of hilarious laughter, the result of some mutual joke which still lay incandescent on the two faces which turned towards them. Joanna ran to meet them.

"Oh, Father, how marvellous, she persuaded you! Tad

says if we hurry I can see his horse before lunch. Just think, he's got a *horse*, right out behind his *house!* I never *knew* a horse, Eve, did you? How do I make friends with him?"

"It's a girl," said Tad. "Name of Christabel. She's partial to a nice chew of carrot now and then."

"Can I *feed* her?"

"If you watch your fingers."

"You see, Father, the minute Eve shows up, the fun begins!" Joanna pointed out, and Eve glanced from her to Tad and back again, tracing the transformation of Joanna in those few minutes from a self-contained young woman resigned to a self-contained hero-worship of Richie Forrest into a radiant, forthcoming girl tiptoe to new experience. Boy meets girl again, Eve thought with astonishment, and added happily, Well, I'll be darned! "I *told* you Eve wouldn't desert us," Joanna was running on recklessly. "I *told* you you'd still get the job! Tad isn't the magazine man, I thought he was, but he lives just over the way, and his sister gives parties, and he has a nephew at Harvard! Father, once Tad had a horse run second at Saratoga! I never saw a real horse race, can we go to Saratoga?" Gradually they had all become conscious that Beau was not entering in. He stood immovable and detached just inside the drawing-room door, so that they would have to pass him to leave the house. His eyes rested on Joanna's new confidence and excitement with an utter disbelief and hostility, which she finally realized and which caused her to fade and droop in mid-flight and brought her to a stand in front of him. Then, with a defiant upward glance at him under her lashes, she said, "My coat's in the hall. Let's go."

"Not today, Joanna."

Eve stiffened with horror, and felt Tad's uneasy glance in her direction. Mutiny. The show-down. Joanna's innocent intoxication at the prospect of escape had upset the apple-cart. Beau couldn't bear to see her go free, after all. He couldn't bear the sudden, transparent infatuation with Tad, nor the open tenderness with which Tad was regarding her, a smiling, proprietary acquiescence almost avuncular, but full of promise. Beau could never bear to lose Joanna. Rather than that, rather even than share her with new friends, he was balking again. He was daring Eve now to carry out the threat which he knew would hurt Joanna almost as much as himself. He thought she couldn't do it. He had called her bluff. He thought even now he could win.

Joanna stood in front of him, looking up.

"You mean you won't come?" she asked quietly.

"Some other time, perhaps."

"Then I'm going without you," said Joanna.

"Not today," he repeated, holding her gaze.

"You've been invited, Father. If you choose not to come that's up to you." And while Eve held her breath,

Joanna turned as if to pass him, and he put out a hand to her arm.

"I'd rather you didn't," he said.

"I'm sorry, Father, but this time I'm going."

"I think not."

They saw his fingers tightened against her pull towards the door so that she swung back on one foot and wrenched herself out of his grasp. Her face was white and quivering, whether with fear or anger neither Eve nor Tad could have told as they stood rooted, watching a battle in which they no longer had any part.

"You can't do it again!" said Joanna. "Eve asked me to go with her the other night, and I stayed because I was sorry for you. I'm *always* sorry for you. But you don't even *try*, Father, it doesn't have to be like this! You don't have to shut yourself up with all that bitterness and despair any longer! You've got the new job you wanted, Eve is willing to be friends, we've got neighbors like Tad, there are things to do, people to know — there's no sense in your living like this, and *I'm* not going to, I'm going to accept every invitation that comes, I'm going to have friends and feed horses and go dancing and — and *fall in love!*" She flashed away from them, through the doorway into the hall.

"Hooray!" cried Tad, following at once. "Count me in — on all of it!"

Eve met Beau's stricken gaze with a small rueful smile.

"You can't blame me for that, Beau. Only yourself. If you hadn't tried to double-cross me nothing like that would have happened. So I didn't have to lift a finger, after all." She went and put an arm through his, determinedly friendly still, and drew him out into the hall. The front door stood open, with sunlight pouring in across the carpet. The other two were already outside, and Joanna was admiring Tad's yellow convertible. "It's not too late, even now," Eve said. "Come to lunch with us. She won't leave you unless you stay behind."

He paused in the shaft of sunshine which fell through the open door. His arm was unresponsive against her side. In the drive, they could see Joanna getting into the seat beside the wheel, and Tad closed the door gently and leaned on it, looking down, while she looked up, and both of them were laughing.

"Coming, Beau?" Eve said patiently.

"Not today," he said again, like a sleep-walker. "I've got something to do here."

"The portrait?"

"What else? It's all there is, isn't it?"

"*No!*" Eve cried violently, and shook him with both hands on his sleeve. "You're so *wrong*, how can you *do* it, Beau, how can you make a prison of love and a curse of grief? You love Joanna, no matter what — you love her so much you devour her, like a spider! Love isn't a shroud, it's a ball-gown! You loved Margie, but still you keep her earthbound by this *pitiless* mourning! There is no virtue in sorrow that suffocates the dead as well as the living! Sure you loved Margie, and she died, and you don't know how to bear it — but don't take it out on her, for God's sake be man enough to bear it *alone*, set her free, *let her go!*"

He was staring at her, stony, impassive, motionless. Her grip on his arm softened remorsefully, and with a brief, apologetic pressure she took her hands away.

"I'm sorry, Beau — forgive me for yelling at you. Shall I go now?"

She waited a moment more, watching his face. He did not move or speak. She left him slowly, and walked to the car. Tad opened the door and she got into the seat beside Joanna. He went around and slid under the wheel and the engine started.

As the car moved away down the drive Eve looked back. The door still stood open, with a wedge of sunlight lying on the carpet inside.

When the sound of the motor had died away Beau turned and went back to the studio. On the easel the portrait waited, unfinished, accusing. It was not Margie. It was not anybody. It was a hopeless daub.

He picked up the paint-stained rag he had dropped before shaking hands with Eve, and soaked it with turpentine from a bottle, and passed it slowly, thoroughly, across the canvas, wiping the colors into one long rainbow smear. And then without looking back he went to the open casement window and leaned there, seeing the empty garden and the sky and white clouds.

And Margie was gone.

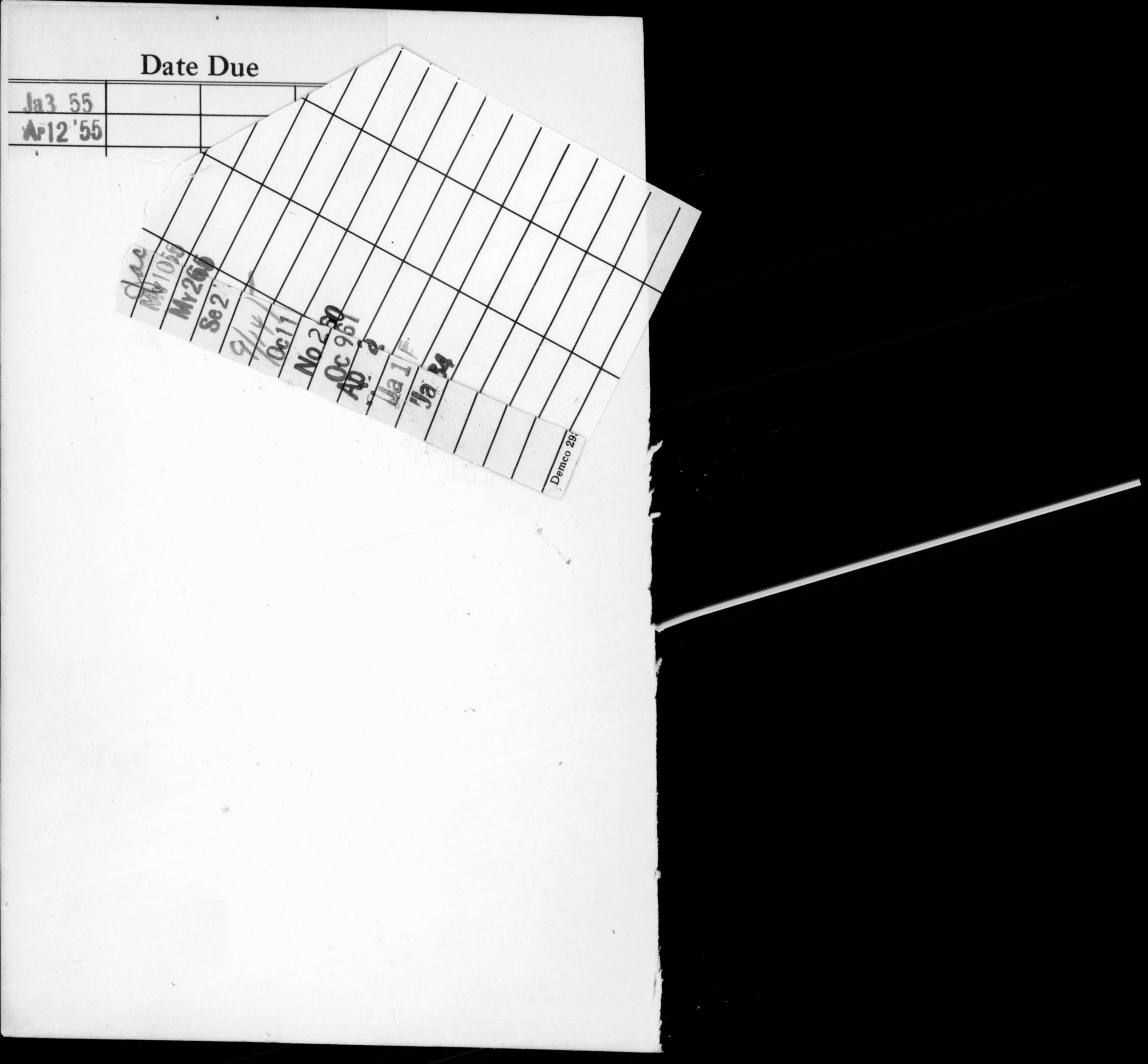